DOWSING THE
UNIVERSE

To My Friend
Pat
Barr

Barbara Sullivan-Nelson

DOWSING THE UNIVERSE

Barbara S. Nelson

A Freedom Promise

TATE PUBLISHING
AND ENTERPRISES, LLC

Published by Tate Publishing & Enterprises, LLC
127 E. Trade Center Terrace | Mustang, Oklahoma 73064 USA
1.888.361.9473 | www.tatepublishing.com

Tate Publishing is committed to excellence in the publishing industry. The company reflects the philosophy established by the founders, based on Psalm 68:11,
"The Lord gave the word and great was the company of those who published it."

Book design copyright © 2013 by Tate Publishing, LLC. All rights reserved.
Cover design by Junriel Boquecosa
Interior design by Caypeeline Casas

Published in the United States of America

ISBN: 978-1-62854-316-2
1. Fiction / General
2. Fiction / Science Fiction / General
13.09.28

DEDICATION

The story is dedicated to the conscientious men and women of the National Aeronautical and Space Agency and of Homeland Security who strive to help humankind increase knowledge and protect our nation and the world. It is also in honor of those who are constantly intrigued by endless curiosity and the possibility of life beyond our planet.

ACKNOWLEDGMENTS

This novel was challenging because I only became as passionately interested in space and life beyond our own world in the process of writing it. Yet, I have always been intrigued by space travel and wanted to develop a story related to it with complex situations.

Every line I have written for years, from responses in newspapers to my last book about a special needs young lady, has helped me meet challenges and increasingly improve my clarity of expression. Those who have made these challenges easier for me deserve credit that cannot be put into words.

To Susan, Sharon, Janet, Rebecca, Brad, and Jim Junior—my children—thanks for your enthusiasm over the years.

To my many friends and relatives, who continue to support and give me confidence.

To my friend and neighbor, Dr. Stephen Collier, thank you for your kindness and wisdom in helping edit this book.

To young Jacob Watson, who suggested the name KEBOW for my aliens.

PROLOGUE

———⟫●⟪———

"DOWSING THE UNIVERSE"

Barbara Sullivan-Nelson

Three female scientists, each initially incarcerated, were given an opportunity of spending a year on a foreign planet. Their intelligence and expertise led to an offer from the United States government, up to the highest level, to offer them exoneration for their crimes after fulfilling a highly classified mission on that planet.

The women learned that a wealthy Russian oligarch, Viktor Stanislaus, was responsible for planning and funding extensive terrorism. The scope of this was a threat to that planet, Europedus, and Earth. The three women were challenged to earn freedom and fuller lives and love as they displayed qualities of courage, bravery and loyalty.

THE FIRST INTERVIEW

It was a foggy early morning with visibility of only about two miles. A conspicuously shy black limousine with government tags traveled down a narrow isolated road. As the marine driver had expected, they approached Central California Women's Correction Facility which was framed by galvanized razor fencing. Close to sixteen feet high, the fencing was very effective, as was obvious to those who knew about those things. The passengers were two men and a woman. Sent on an extremely unusual mission, they were to visit one of the inmates.

The government regarded the mission with top security and priority. The three, highly trained scientists were sent to interview one Geena McBride. McBride, a thirty-one-year-old botanist was serving a life sentence for murder.

Dressed in loosely fitting grey denim coveralls with an identification number stenciled on the front bodice, Geena McBride was taking a scheduled break in the activities yard when the car arrived. The air was a cool fifty-six degrees on this November morning but promised to reach sixty-eight or so the meteorologists predicted.

"They're here," the warden's message for someone assigned to summon Geena McBride was brief.

Geena picked up her pace as she strode down the immaculate, pale green corridor. Ignoring the stares of fellow inmates returning from the activities yard as she headed to Warden Post's office, Geena muttered to herself, "What could people from NASA possibly want with me?"

A carefully limited amount of information had been shared before the meeting. That left much room for speculation. As she knocked on the door, she recalled several visits to the warden's office to discuss disputes and concerns among the inmates. Geena was a trained scientist with an earned doctorate. This had meant little to most around her but had probably led her logical mind, combined with her compassionate nature, to gain respect from most of the prison personnel and an impressive number of inmates.

"Please come in," Warden Post instructed. After recognizing Geena's slender form through the frosty and bulletproof glass, she released the lock.

Warden Carole Post was a stern but compassionate woman in her late fifties. Taller than Geena's five-foot-four height, she appeared a bit stocky, with faded blond hair. Not at all the stereotype of a prison warden, she was respected and dedicated, striving to help rehabilitate all the inmates during their time there.

Geena was puzzled as two men in black business suits and a woman in a conservative navy suit greeted her. The three officers in the military, dressed as civilians, were also scientists.

After the introductions, Warden Post continued, "These people are trained scientists sent by the National Aeronautical and Space Administration to discuss an important and highly classified project."

In some confusion and puzzlement, Geena looked at the warden. "Why would you want to talk to me?"

After further introductions by name and area of specialty, they began to present some details for a project so farfetched to be imaginable.

"What are you saying? That you may want to send me into space?" Geena questioned incredulously.

The younger man, Dr. Donald Clark, was slender, light complexioned and had almost boyish looks. "Would you like to hear more?"

"Are you for real? Yes, of course, I want to hear more," she uttered and quietly listened.

The visitors elaborated about a recent finding of the *Cassini* probe while orbiting Saturn. One of Saturn's smaller moons, previously considered uninhabitable, may actually have water and an atmosphere conducive to life, possibly even human life.

Dr. Clark continued, "According to our best determination so far, this small planet-like moon, which we now call Europedus, is the size of Texas. It has a likely gravity similar to that on Earth. Preliminary findings suggest that the surface temperature ranges are similar to that of Earth in tested areas."

"What do you mean by tested areas? How are they tested?" Geena quickly asked.

Dr. Edward Garn, a sophisticated tall man with dark hair and graying temples was a renowned scientist, medical doctor, and former astronaut. He replied, "An area tested by robotic equipment from a space launch this past July indicates strongly that human life, as well as plant life, can and indeed may exist. The Kepler Mission confirms this."

Geena remembered reading about this mission named for Dr. Johannes Kepler. The Kepler Mission is NASA's search for planets with Earth like qualities.

"There is a network of motion sensors or seismometers which were left on the surface. They have indicated tiny movements. Laser reflectors have also helped us decide on further research needed. One of the main goals of this next project will be determining how many layers are under the first crust of the rock surface," Dr. Garn continued.

Geena quickly recalled that the Earth has three main layers, a crust of rock, a mantle of denser rock, and the final layer, a core containing large amounts of iron. She knew that some scientists believed that Mars may have similar layers. Obviously, however, she knew water was essential to any planet being able to support Earth-like life.

The woman was Dr. Gretchen Von Goethe, a short woman possibly appearing to look younger than her age. Yet she speaks with unembellished authority and confidence. "According to a recent find by astrobiologists, there may have been water, vapor or other fluid spewing from Europedus. From what we have conjectured, there may be an ocean or other large body of water under that moon's crust," Dr. Van Goethe suggested.

Geena felt that Dr. Von Goethe was bright, cultured, and accomplished. "What does that mean?"

Geena observed Dr. Von Goethe as a woman around forty years old. The petite woman spoke with a quiet but commanding authority of power. Geena saw in her a refined, cultured, and charming, woman, defending her non-fashionable appearance by her position. She detected a somewhat earthy woman obscured by definition of profession. *She would look better without her hair tied in a bun*, Geena thought to herself. What came to her mind is a quote by Milton: "Mine outward semblance doth deceive the truth."

Young Dr. Clark interrupted as if he were reading a textbook quote, "We have learned plumes of water spewing into space indicate the possibility that an ocean lies hidden under that moon's crust. The origin of internal heat needed to fire this plume of water or vapor, remains a mystery."

Geena envisioned him as articulate and driven to achieve. "Is this an indication of life on the planet?" she asked.

"It is yet to be fully determined," he replied. "If there is any life on this moon or planet we call Europedus, it will, no doubt, be very primitive. Our goal is to send qualified personnel to areas such as this to gain further information and determine what this might mean."

"Does this mean that I might be among those who get to go?"

"If you qualify and have the aptitude, confidence, and will to succeed, the answer is yes."

Dr. Von Goethe spoke again. "We must tell you that this is a dangerous mission. You will be at great risk."

Geena leaned back in her chair as she let out a very long sigh. As she brushed her long golden-red hair away from her face, she tried to wrap her mind around all that this meant. They all waited in silence, observing her every reaction

Dr. Von Goethe continued, "If chosen, the United States government has committed to grant you complete restitution after completing the mission and returning to Earth. This will likely require one year there or until which time your assignment is satisfactorily deemed complete. NASA and the Department of Homeland Security will make this determination. There will be no record of your incarceration."

"That is"—Geena looks at them one by one as the Warden remained silent—"assuming I am lucky enough to return to Earth, right?" Her eyebrows rose as if waiting for an answer.

Silence deafened the room, speaking the obvious. Warden Post glanced at Geena, as all waited for someone else to address the issue. Geena glared at the three, "I called that one correctly. I'm sure." After breathing deeply, with concern and anticipation, Geena declared, "I don't seem to have much of a future here. What are my chances of becoming one who is chosen?"

Dr. Clark raced to answer as the other two continued to take notes. "We're aware of your skills, expertise, and knowledge. These are definite pluses. However, we cannot make any promises at this time."

"You have obviously done your homework about my background."

"Yes," he admitted, "we have been following you for quite some time. We even have your birth and dental records."

"Well, that puts a bite on things," she commented, displaying her usual quick humor. "Who are the other committee members for this project?" Uneasiness and concern for details was evident in some tightness to her voice and her facial muscles.

Dr. Gretchen Von Goethe or Dr. VG, as her counterparts called her, explained, "There are nine members who will make the final selections. They include the three of us. Others include members of Congress from both the House and Senate, a representative from the Department of Homeland Security, and the president of the United States."

The three had been visibly pleased with this initial meeting with Geena. They indicated that one year on Europedus was only part of the program. "We are not at liberty to discuss the entire program at this time," Dr. Garn explained. "Even we, are not privy to the complete project, nor do we have authority to speculate".

Geena's assessment of him gained further appreciation. She recalled another astronaut with a similar name. "Are you related to Sen. Edwin Garn, whom, I think, was aboard the *Discovery* a few years ago?"

"No. He was a fine man with a good name but no relation to me," Dr. Garn replied.

After two hours of extensive discussion, the meeting concluded. The visitors collected their data, picked up their briefcases, and cordially said their good-byes as they approached the door, Dr. Garn in the lead. He turned briefly and made one parting comment. "We cannot stress enough the importance of keeping the contents of this and future meetings within these four walls."

They all agreed, including Warden Post, as the three repeated their good-byes and a hint of possible return.

Geena and Warden Post watched out the window in silence, as the departing three figures, escorted through the security gates, disappeared into another world—a world of potential and promise. Geena was intrigued and fascinated by the possibilities and vowed to keep learning as much as she could about this mission whether chosen to participate or not.

With almost a tear in her eye, Geena suggested to Warden Post, "I am excited about this proposal. It might indeed be a chance to live a free and normal life again. It is overwhelming to think I might be able to help the world in a place that is, pardon the pun, absolutely out of this world."

Warden Post looked at Geena with both hope and sympathy. "I know it is, Geena, if that is what you want. If it becomes reality it will be your chance of a lifetime—a dangerous chance of a lifetime!"

Her background as a marine had enabled the warden to effectively work at her challenging job yet also helped her be purposeful and direct. We must keep this under wraps," she directed to Geena, who responded in complete agreement. "Who would believe it anyway?"

Once again, Geena cursed the day she married Thomas McBride, her former supervisory professor in Georgia State. "I didn't listen to the warnings, even my own feelings," she grumbled. "I honestly didn't want to know all the answers. I was too captivated by the romance of forbidden involvement, clandestine meetings, beguiled by his authority and, initially, his charming manner and looks. Of course, it's too late to dwell on what might have been."

Warden Post gave her a sympathetic glance as she escorted Geena to the door leading into the common hallway of cells.

Shivering with waves of excitement, Geena prompted her way down the long hallway to the confinement of a small chamber she referred to as the dorm. As many voices competed to ask what is going on with her being gone most of the afternoon, she replied with expressionless mirth, "The warden wanted my opinion about including a swimming pool and spa in the west wing."

Laughter came from all around as a matron unlocked her cell while making jokes to review again at the mess table. Her sense of humor had again helped enable Geena to live and not just subsist during her confinement.

This encounter with the NASA officials prompted many memories. *It has been quite a roller coaster*, she reflected. As a young child, losing both parents in a tragic accident, she went to live with her maternal Grandmother in England. There, her shared interest with her grandmother on all sorts of plants quickly ignited a passion to learn and apply as much as she could. Her educational goals were launched. She subsequently developed a passion for plant life along with her grandmother whom she adored. Upon graduating with highest honors from Cambridge, she determined to explore where she and her father were born. Returning to the United States and enrolling at Georgia State, she completed two years of postgraduate work.

During that time, she became involved with one of her professors, Thomas McBride. An opportunity to leave Georgia and study at the famed Kazan Institute at the University of Moscow seemed like a dream. Here was a chance to study with the best of botanists, astronomers, and linguists at the Kazan, widely acknowledged as the "Birthplace of Organic Chemistry," providing the very best opportunity to hone her knowledge and skills.

As Geena sometimes confided to only her closest friends, "This opportunity to study at Kazan came at just the right time. Guess I was getting too involved with Tom."

While at Kazan, Geena became fluent in Russian, bringing her a great deal of confidence and satisfaction. Her academic zeal and energy reached ever higher levels of success.

"My major downfall was going back to Georgia to marry Tom. After we were married, the abuse began. I had so much to live for and threw it all away."

Back in Atlanta, she became the director of an endowed scientific museum center. Her supervisors were among her most ardent supporters. As one quickly indicated, "Dr. McBride's knowledge of devices and instruments of science, her expertise and passion for excellence are beyond compare."

<hr />

Imprisoned in 2001, Geena McBride was one of several hundred women incarcerated at the Central California Facility, the largest female correctional institution in the United States. It opened in 1990 and covered over 640 acres. As indicated by their mission statement, the determination of their warden, and the carefully instilled training of correctional officers and other employees, they do not want to just house the inmates. They seem to really want to embody the statement: "The primary mission of the (CCWF) is to process and incarcerate California's female offenders in a secure, safe, disciplined, and ethical institutional setting." They considered conditions or actions that rendered either correctional officers or inmates to be totally unacceptable.

One of the programs available to the inmates was a battered women's support group. Geena was a productive contributor to this as well as being an object lesson herself. Convicted of killing her husband, she especially wanted to be involved in the program.

When applying to Warden Carole Post, she noted, "California has the unenviable distinction of having the most women prisoners in the nation. I would like to be instrumental in reducing the number of repeat offenders. Lecturing the importance of alternatives to avoid consequences is so important to me."

Her subsequent conduct and statements rewarded Warden Post's confidence in Geena as she became invaluable in inmate issue discussions and feedback.

SECOND INTERVIEW

The next interview took place a few weeks later in December at the Valley State Prison for Women, the smaller of two women's prisons near Chowchilla, south of Merced, in Central California. Designed to accommodate fewer than four thousand prisoners, the facility opened in 1995 on a 640-acre site in the San Joaquin Valley.

Marcie Adams, a twenty seven-year-old Harvard trained physicist, was the second woman chosen to be interviewed. At five foot six, with short light-brown hair, she reminded them of the girl next door. As a professor teaching at a local college in Boulder, Colorado, Marcie also mastered and then taught karate and other martial arts. Like Geena, she was intrigued at the idea that anyone from NASA would travel to talk with her, especially now and in prison.

"Marcie, tell us about yourself and why you are here." As she considered how to reply, speculation that this might have something to do with an assignment offered to her by NASA years ago crowded her thoughts.

"I was educated as an atomic-nuclear physicist and worked as a mission scientist at the space institute in Boulder."

"We have learned you were quite skilled and respected by your peers and supervisors," Dr. Garn began.

"Yes! I did enjoy my work there tremendously until the Boulder campus at the University of Colorado recruited me to teach. I saw it as a wonderful opportunity."

All three looked a bit surprised, but, it is Dr. Von Goethe who asked, "Why would you give up a promising and prestigious career to teach?"

"I can only acknowledge that wonderful teachers who inspired me no doubt influenced that decision."

Garn, Clark, and Von Goethe all silently listened to her reply. Almost simultaneously, the three inquired. "What led to your prison conviction?"

"At the university, I became addicted to my own physico-chemical compounds from the experiments I had devised. I was arrested on school property, charged, and, after conviction, was dubbed a felon."

"Why would you do such a thing?"

"My mother had been diagnosed with a rare type of cancer. I was arrogant and headstrong enough to think I could discover a cure or help in some significant way."

"What were your credentials before Boulder?"

"My stepfather is a physician. I absorbed as many of his medical texts all through my younger years and graduated from college in Chicago. Once accepted in the medical program and then post residency at Harvard. I knew I always wanted to be involved in medicine. When offered an opportunity to work in Santa Barbara, it was as a member of very advanced medical application in experimental contexts. NASA contacted me about an opening to work as a specialist at the institute in Boulder. I did that for a while, but nothing intrigued me for long as much as the desire to teach. That is why I spent more and more time as a chemistry professor and mentor researcher at the Boulder campus.

"Did your stepfather mentor you?"

"Yes, he has always been extremely encouraging and support-ive, but not, of course, with those contraband experiments. All he wanted was for me to be successful and happy. I should have listened when he tried to help me face what I so fiercely resisted. I didn't want to accept that there was no cure for my mother. I gained all this wonderful education and experience but seemed to have developed the simplicity of a moron. I fear that I have become my own worst enemy."

Dr. Garn, impressed by her frankness and candid analy-sis, thought to himself; *she is such an attractive young woman, apparently inside as well as her appearance. How sad that this has all happened.* Like Geena, Marcie looked nothing at all like a typical criminal. Fit, but not muscle bound, she reminded them again of the proverbial girl next door. "According to Amnesty International, convictions for drug offenses account for one in three of all women serving time in prison," Dr. Garn noted.

Sorrowfully and barely uttering, Marcie admitted, "I made a serious mistake, and now I am one of those statistics."

"Marcie, tell us about your experiences living in prison," Dr. Garn requested. "We know that this is not a life sentence, but twenty-five years is long enough for you to have considered alter-natives? Have you ever thought of suicide?"

Tearful eyes met his in shocked amazement. "My imprison-ment hasn't been a walk in the park, but to throw away my life and any possibility of a future is out of the question. That would be the ultimate crime. Your possible assignment for me may be the best positive news I have been able to consider."

"What about the unpleasantry and abuse that you spoke of in prison?"

"Harassing one another over jealousies and petty differences is a familiar pastime of women inmates as well as a few of the correctional officers. The fact that I am an expert in karate has no doubt helped me to protect myself. This has probably helped in making a few friends. Yet avoiding the troublemakers is a full-time task. Fortunately, many of the women like to hear the sound of their own voices, not leading to violence most of the time."

"How are the day-to-day living conditions and activities?"

"The food isn't gourmet, but most of the time is satisfactory. I get plenty of exercise since I know tai chi and other ways to strive to stay fit, even when in the cell. I have extensive computer and library privileges. Other than that, it is a place to meditate and think. Perhaps that is the biggest mixed blessing. I wonder why I was so tempted and vulnerable. I deeply regret what I did, especially what brought disgrace to the school and students."

Clark, Garn, and Von Goethe alternated in providing the same basic preliminary information given to Geena McBride. Since Marcie Adams had been with NASA before, some of the detailed specifics varied, but with the same caveats and slight limitations on full disclosure, they shared with her what was to be involved if selected for the mission.

She listened and asked questions for over two more hours. As the three described the process of the selection committee's assignment and choices, she is cautiously excited about this possibility.

"I am certainly flattered and especially impressed with the president's involvement, but I'm not sure if I'm qualified for such a mission," she told them. "I hadn't seriously considered myself as one going into space."

However, she had impressed the three interviewers as not only physically fit and knowledgeable, but also capable of learning quickly and well. Impressed by Marcie and her qualifications, the three were confident that her reluctance was temporary.

There was obvious agreement as they left the prison.

"I believe in this one and feel we can gain her full involvement if the committee approves," Dr. Garn commentated.

Dr. Von Goethe announced with confidence, "She has my vote."

Dr. Clark concurred.

A THIRD CANDIDATE

Another month went by as the search continued. As the three interviewers scrutinized various prison records and memoranda, they rejected twelve candidates. They realized this is not for lack of education and apparent qualifications and obviously not lack of availability.

"It is both surprising and depressing how many intelligent, educated people are incarcerated," comments Dr. Clark.

Dr. Garn agreed with disappointment. "Some women, otherwise qualified, excluded themselves by giving up on themselves not having kept mentally or physically fit.

Finally, they traveled to a smaller prison in Central Florida and encountered Angela Hastings. Angela had been working for a NASA facility as an astronomer when her abusive husband fell asleep after a night of drunken rage. After this final bout of abuse, which followed repeated efforts to gain protection for herself, she locked herself in the closet while he ranted and raved. She was about to leave the house while he slept, but not before turning the gas burners of the stove on. When her husband awakened, he lit a cigarette. According to the authorities, "There was quite a fireworks display."

Angela, a petite African-American woman, at thirty years old, had been a victim of abuse and neglect from childhood. This became a pattern for her. She faced abuse while being raised in her Aunt Cora's home and later into her teens in a foster home. This is all related to the interviewers when Angela was asked to tell them about herself.

"My mother died when I was an infant, leaving me with her sister. She didn't really want me and managed to find a foster family. They permitted someone to abuse me and take advantage of me for many years. Finally, I was fortunate. A neighbor, a gentle soul, a retired pastor, rescued me, enabled me to finish high school and go to college. His name was the Reverend Jacob Morrison. I called him Pop. He was a godsend for me, like a grandfather. At the time of his death, I had just received a full scholarship to the University of Chicago's Department of Astronomy and Astrophysics. Pop left me his entire estate. I was his only family, he would often say."

As she continued her story without interruption, the three interviewers listened in reverence to her fight for survival and power to succeed.

Angela was composed and undisturbed as she continued. "Life was good until I met and later married a smooth-talking mobster who described himself as a business executive from downtown Chicago."

She elaborated a bit more about her marriage with obvious sorrow. Yet, she was especially eager to talk with the interviewers. Angela had heard rumors about a possible program in which they were obviously capable of being involved. That they had come to consider her for such a confidential mission fascinated her. Friends at NASA with whom she still had some contact had given her both information and speculation, so obviously, imaginations became involved. She knew something was up; perhaps she might even be asked for advice or expertise, she thought.

Acknowledging her ultimate responsibility for her incarceration, Angela still conveyed remorse. Continued abuse from her husband was a logical, if not legal, reason for less-severe punishment perhaps. Yet she was at least partially accepting she was culpable and where she belonged.

"Before long, I suspected my husband of dealing in drugs. It was obvious that he was a user himself. Begging him to stop, to turn himself in, and to seek help, he increased his screaming and began hitting, even pistol-whipping me. That was the last straw. He was a large, commanding man, and I was increasingly afraid of him. It became even more difficult that he had been so caring and seemed to have such a good side initially. His mood could change at the slightest irritation," she continued with candor.

"I turned the gas on the stove without a flame and left the house for what I intended to be a short period. I guess I wanted to make him nauseous, sick enough to go for help, maybe even the hospital. Of course, I was going to get back and turn the gas off but was unexpectedly detained by a nearby traffic accident." She continued with a deep breath or two to regain more composure. "I was sentenced to life without parole for premeditated murder and have spent the last three years in this prison."

"Angela," Dr. Von Goethe quietly asked, "why didn't you alert the authorities of these suspected drug connections when you asked for protection?"

"I had no proof. I was desperately afraid of him and of his connections. No doubt, he would have killed me or had someone else kill me. By that time, I was a threat to him and, in his words, "expendable."

As they had with Geena and Marcie, it was difficult for the interviewers not to be sympathetic to Angela, this most recent of their candidates. They asked if she had any questions and explained to her, there are limitations of what they are authorized to reveal. Thanking her for her time, they packed up their notes and prepared to leave the facility.

"Thank you so much," Angela uttered. "I look forward to hearing from you."

Angela's experiences and intuition had helped her read between the lines. It seemed obvious to her that something amazing might become involved for her on one level or another.

From her perspective, the interviewers were impressed with the education, levels of accomplishment, and related apparent potential of each of the three who, in their minds, at least, were excellent candidates for this assignment. Although not their final decision, Geena, Marcie, and Angela were all vetted for further consideration.

A HEAVENLY OPPORTUNITY

The larger selection committee ultimately confirmed the three women the interviewers had proposed. A contract was prepared to offer Geena McBride, Marcie Adams, and Angela Hastings assignments for the mission. All committee members concurred. The next step would be the acceptance of the three women.

Once explained, each of the three had been both cautiously skeptical and extremely anxious for more information. It was explained that if they agreed and fulfilled this assignment to participate in a scientific mission outside of the Earth's atmosphere, possibly up to a full year or until the project was deemed complete, they could anticipate exoneration for their respective crimes by the United States government. The quick concern of one of the women that some of these were state, rather than federal, concerns that were alleviated by the United States justice department's specialist who liaison with state governors.

Another significant concern was about the likelihood of returning to Earth safely. Separately, each agreed to listen further and gain as much information as possible. After a month, which involved briefings and even more extensive background checks and clearances, the three united at a secret Florida location. Psychologists, internists, and other specialists interviewed them as orientation for their assignments began.

Dr. James Monroe addressed them in what seemed a small classroom. "Ladies, from today forward, I want you to think of yourselves as astronauts. You already have the physical attributes and potential to be trained and successful. One of our goals is to help you reach those levels."

Monroe was about fifty years old, with gray-white temples and moustache. He had the look of an academic and fulfilled that role in increasingly responsible research-and-teaching assignments at several universities. His primary expertise was in psychiatry, neuropsychology, and brain development. "I will be with you through much of the next few weeks. If any of you have concerns about your participation in this mission, now is the time to discuss it," he instructed. As all three began to talk at once, he remarked, "Marcie, I will start with you. Please feel free to say anything you wish to."

"I am very excited to be involved, and I believe in this mission, but I'm not as confident about my part. I question my own abilities," Marcie replied.

"How about you, Geena? And you, Angela?"

Both agreed with Marcie's succinct concerns. None of the three was reticent to admit what had been tantamount to their thoughts.

For a long moment, Dr. Monroe looked at each and their expressions. Finally, he spoke. "I would seriously be worried if you didn't have those feelings. This is actually a good thing. I can assure you, by the time you are ready to leave Earth, each of you will think you could do it by yourself if need be."

They each had reservations that this would ever be true but laughed at the thought. He had encouraged them to speak, to express their thoughts and questions, not just listen.

The six-hour session actually went quickly for them. "Ladies, this is it for today. Tomorrow's time will be somewhat shorter because I have prior commitments in the early afternoon," Dr. Monroe reminded.

Escorted back to their individual quarters, they shared many positive comments about the day and Dr. Monroe. It was Angela who remarked, "Isn't it wonderful to be treated as a productive member of society again?"

Several days later, they were introduced to Captain Guy Sterling, a marine, who was on special assignment with NASA to work with them.

"Ladies, I know you are all highly knowledgeable, and every report has indicated your capabilities and potential. Our objective is to hone and fine-tune your skills for what we plan. While on this mission, you are to study and collect samples. This will entail liquids, such as water, and soil, rock, plant life, insects, anything of that type you encounter. Be sure to keep careful analysis on your computer modules, and we don't object to back up notes you deem appropriate. We want to analyze and learn all we can. Be sure to forward your analyses, even speculations, to Mission Control on a regular basis.

"You will be using some very special equipment, some of which was developed just for this project but will, no doubt, open significant areas of future knowledge. Before you leave, you will become acquainted with much of this equipment. This is where I come in. My expertise is in developing and training others to make the best use of it."

Marcie couldn't help but notice what a skillful speaker he was, aside from his dashing good looks. Captain Sterling concluded the introduction with a summary of his professional career. All three of the women noticed the shiny gold band on his left hand.

"Captain Sterling?" Angela intoned.

"Yes, Angela," he replied.

"Can you give us more insight how and why this project began?"

"Yes, and why send three convicted felons?" Geena quickly urged.

"We are confident you three ladies have the knowledge and expertise which is needed and, if you forgive me, have the time to spare. NASA has extensive information already about a small planet named Europedus. Originally thought one of the uninhabitable bodies in space, now there is speculation this may not be the case. We need to learn much more about it, and the present administration, the Department of Defense, and NASA are collaborating in training and supporting you to do that. That's almost as much as I am privy to myself, ladies. The rest of the details remain a mystery to me as much as to you."

What Captain Sterling declined to divulge was the existence of other dangers. Specifically, either dangers to the planet from Earth or dangers to Earth from the planet, may not be out of the question. Behind all these were competing rumors from a Russian national-security team, an agency from the United Nations, and other organizations having been flummoxed in efforts to learn details.

In consultation with their counterparts in the United States, the Russian government had revealed the existence of such threats. Captain Sterling knew that thwarting such from either direction will be revealed as part of this mission. *The women are not ready to learn this yet*, he willingly decided.

Carefully choosing his words, Captain Sterling continued, "In a practical world, an idea of sending three women, convicted felons or not, to such an environment for research wouldn't be considered. However, after our investigation and your training, we are confident this mission should succeed. Remember that you are to no longer think of yourselves as felons, but as newly minted or soon-to-be-trained astronauts. This is what you are, and this is how I perceive each of you."

PHYSICAL TRAINING PROCESS

An exhaustive physical-training preparation was ongoing. The next six months provided mind-numbing, almost-grueling lessons, experiments, and training to all three women. Although some hints about the mission leaked to the media, the details and all locations of activity remained carefully concealed from the public. The three "inmates," as they themselves, failed to erase that word from their minds, continued subsequent training on a private island off the coast of Florida. Each had her own tent, but they studied, trained, and ate together.

Beside an ongoing security detail and periodic visits from dieticians, Marine Corps physical-training specialists, and scientific experts were the others on the island. Not serious about it, the women acknowledged that only two options exist for escaping the island: *slim* and *none*. The water surrounding was alligator-infested and quite deep. The only access was by boat or helicopter. A portion of land cleared for the helipad, where they landed, permitted others to come and go. Boats were disallowed in the area for the time NASA had requisitioned the island's use. Arrangement for a doctor, triage team, or other specialists to be on call from Miami's Mount Sinai Hospital was a precaution in the event of an emergency. They too would have arrived by helicopter if needed.

In the heat and humidity of the area, efforts to limit physical exercise to the cooler times of day became even more difficult.

There didn't seem to be any of that. With studies, research, and exercise, they were typically exhausted by nightfall. Yet the counselors who assisted Dr. James Monroe in analyzing and evaluating their progress agreed with him that the women were doing well.

"They appear to be developing a sisterhood. Each of the three reflects an excellent attitude. They seem to be reclaiming a sense of self-confidence and pride. Two of them have mentioned the possibility of marrying and raising a family."

Dr. Jim, as they thought of him among themselves, had often reminded them of something, which had brought confidence and hope. "Jesus knows how you feel—hurt, scared, and alone. He promises to always be with you, to wrap you in the comfort of His love. And remember what we read in Genesis, "I am with you and will watch over you wherever you go and I will bring you back to this land. I will not leave you until I have done what I have promised you."

Their training continued as the women gained physical strength and even more self-assurance. They also learned about one another and about their shared values.

Dr. Monroe scrutinized all evaluations and forwarded progress reports to Mission Control. He remarked, "All three women are evaluated constantly for scientific expertise, general knowledge, physical skills, and attitude. All three continue to progress well in every area."

⟶⟶⊷⊶⟵⟵

Perhaps shared concerns and involvement had nurtured complete confidence among Geena, Marcie, and Angela. Almost too busy to reflect on anything else but assignments at hand, sometimes the reasons for their incarceration still came to mind for any one of the women. It was Marcie who shared how becoming involved in experiments in which she was, herself, a human guinea pig led to her crime.

"I began inducing small amounts of controlled substances in various combinations. I hoped this would lead to more permanent remission, if not even possibly a cure for my mother's melanoma. My experiments had undertaken a life of their own. I got caught up in both a desperate effort to succeed and the thrill of potential discovery."   As her eyes welled up, she continued, "Some of my students became aware of what I was doing, although I did not actually involve any of them. Their parents and the university authorities were incensed that I would jeopardize any students or do such things, much less on school property. The university saw it as a potential liability, of course.

"About that time, Mother died. I was devastated and felt my experimental failures even more keenly. I not only let my mother down, I let the school and the students down. Many were very close to me and attempted to present testimony in my behalf at the sentencing. Nevertheless, I was exhausted and didn't even do much for my own defense. It's almost a blessing that Mother didn't live to see her only child imprisoned. My stepfather stays in touch. He's been a supportive, loving parent for as long as I can remember."

"What about your biological father?" Geena asked.

"He died in a boating accident when I was an infant, leaving Mother with mounting debts. She remarried when I was three. My stepfather provided us with a wonderful life, materially and emotionally."

With a lump in her throat, she continued, "He is the only father I can remember. Perhaps because he is a physician, I gained an early passion for learning all kinds of things. He helped me become interested in all sciences, especially geology and astronomy. By taking this chance, I hope to make him proud. It broke his heart when I was sent to prison."

Morning arrived too soon. Yet the three women were becoming acclimated to the regime and steamy weather. One particular morning, however, fierce lightning and powerful gusts of wind awakened them. Yet the training continued. At one point, a large falling tree, struck by lightning, almost struck Angela as it fell.

"Fortunately, I saw it at the last moment and was able to get out of the way," she later remarked.

"We saw that," Geena replied with admiration. "Guess we'll have to call you the Gazelle—you responded so swiftly and well." Amazingly, Angela applied her trained physical skills and escaped with only minor scuffs and bruises.

Any one of the women could have likely revealed similar skills. Their training reflected even more effects that were positive. However, because of potential threats of more "static discharge," as the lightning related in the subsequent report, they took time off when the weather was particularly threatening.

The falling tree may, have inspired later conversation, when the focus turned to Geena McBride and her background.

"Geena, how did you become so interested in plants?" Angela asked.

"My grandmother lives in England. When my parents died and I went to live with her, we would always spend as much time as possible in her flower garden. She called it her special botanical garden. With little formal education in the area, she nonetheless read everything she could find and studied on her own and became a skilled horticulturist. I especially remember her magnificent rose bushes of every color you can imagine. Even now, while quite a bit older, she seems to connect with plant life. With her, I felt my own kinship to that specialty."

"Did you marry someone in that field of study?" Marcie asked.

"I married one of my former professors after leaving college. He was twice divorced, which should have given me a clue. I was impressed by his maturity and expertise. Then he was considered a highly skilled botanist. Things were fine until he became abusive."

"Was he abusive to his former wives?" Angela asked quickly, hoping Geena would elaborate.

"He was! One of them testified on my behalf during the trial. She was quite convincing, telling the jury details of his abusive personality and how he had acted during his escalating efforts to justify his anger. Her testimony was impressive, but I think the jury wanted to make me an example."

Fascinated by her sorrowful testimony, the other two inquired, almost in unison, "How was he killed?"

"I had begun sleeping with a knife under the mattress. When he came home drunk after a night out with the so-called boys, he started to hit me the second or maybe the third time, each more horrible than the last. I guess I just lost it and stabbed him in the neck."

"Ouch!" Angela exclaimed as she and Marcie looked at one another.

Geena continued the memories as if it were a terrible dream. "The prosecutor kept insisting that my husband was asleep when I attacked him. In the result, the prosecutor was more convincing than my attorney was. I would recommend before a woman marries that she interview a first wife, if she exists, or, in my case, the first and second. I wish I had."

"Three months has been a long time to stay out in the wild, sleeping in a tent and waking up every morning to mind and body numbing exercise," Angela reminded them. "However, we have endured this training so far. We have survived and even thrived." They agreed. "Compared to what we might expect later, this might be like a vacation." Geena gibed to all of them.

They're gratefully pleased with the levels of further knowledge achieved, and this was shared by the program's supervisors. Evaluations uniformly reflected this with appreciation of their attitudes, knowledge, and abilities. Dr. Jim reminded them that he is always available as a sounding board as well as trainer and mentor.

In one of their rare breaks of exhaustive study, research and training, Geena asked, "What about you, Angela, you haven't really elaborated about what happened to put you in prison. Will you tell us?"

Geena and Marcie both looked with intent concern for Angela's reply.

"I turned on the gas of our range and blew the flame out just to make him sick. I didn't think about him awakening to light a cigarette before I got back to turn the burners off and air out the house. When I came around the corner after that traffic mishap that delayed me, flames were shooting out of the roof. Firefighters had taken his body out, but it was too late to save him. I learned that the explosion had killed him."

Geena couldn't help think to herself how amusing this would be to an outsider if it weren't so tragic, especially for her new friend Angela.

Angela began to cry as she added, "The house burned completely".

"Angela, are you okay?" the other two asked in sympathy.

"Yes, I can't help but regret now that what happened had never happened. I should have left him but I was afraid of him. I knew he would follow me."

At that point, Geena's immediate talent for humor prompted her to say, "This once again, proves what a hazard cigarette smoking can be to your health."

Marcie concealed a faint grin.

Angela continued. "He saw me as a threat when I was out of his sight. He knew I suspected him of drug dealing. Turning the gas on was out of desperation. I wanted everyone to know how dangerous a situation I was living in. The forensic pathologist ruled his death a suicide, but somehow or other, word got out that I confessed to having turned on the gas burners. After that, the prosecutor had a field day. It was reelection time, and he wanted to be prominent in the news. He got his wish, and I got life."

"How horrible," both Geena and Marcie gasped. "Do you ever wish you had not confessed that to anyone?"

"Yes, constantly, especially the day I stepped into a cell. I had lost several friends at work and many neighbors, although most understood and a few testified as character witnesses before the sentencing. I loved astronomy, and my work even included assignments with NASA. These, no doubt, led to contacts letting me know the rumors about this mission. My friends at NASA were and remain supportive and active as the only family I have now."

"It appears that we will be a family for quite a while," Marcie and Geena agreed.

———⇒✦⇐———

Many among the old hands at the Florida space center strived to hide their skepticism; at least no one seemed to comment openly. Some of the residual sexism and concern that the women had not come up through the system as most astronauts had, was voiced. Just how competent will these three be? Yet, as Geena Angela and Marcie were to confront new levels of challenge, these obstacles would actually further prepare them. Dr. James Monroe's evaluation summarized their experiences. "They refuse to be intimidated and once again prove skillful achievement and progress," he observed.

They had earned respect from just about everyone with whom they had studied and trained. A typical response, if not often expressed, concerned the evidence that nature had been kind to all three of these women. Each displayed quick intellect and charming personalities that complimented their physical attractiveness.

After over a year of structured training, the three former inmates readied for a final demonstration, confirming they were prepared. A rare nighttime launch, scheduled for May 2 under a full moon, caused the entire area to become excited.

In case of unfavorable weather, an alternate date was set for a few days later. Dr. Jim was on hand to wish them luck and provide his personal farewells. "Ladies, this is where I get off. It has been a delight to get to know and work with each of you. You have earned my respect. You know now, as I do, that you can succeed. I have faith in you and know that with God's guidance and our best wishes, you will be safe. That includes your safe return." They all embraced him as they tearfully bid farewell to him as their primary educator and confidant, one who had become a friend as well.

The past few days had witnessed constant updates to their training and briefing. Constant reminders given to expect the unexpected.

Meeting the others accompanying them on the mission, preliminary introductions were brief. Commander Harris Connelly, who conveyed authority and confidence, headed them. His crew of seven, which included the three women, was fitted with flight suits and related equipment. They were all escorted to the moonlit shuttle, which quietly sat on the launch pad.

THE LIFT OFF

As they reflected on the past year, all three women were quietly impressed by what they had already accomplished. Yet controlled nervousness and logical uncertainty of what was right before them occupied many of their thoughts as well. They agreed that whatever the outcome, the experience had been wonderful. However, they were determined to do their best and succeed.

"We're ready!" Commander Connelly's announcement brought a sudden coldness to Angela's body. Geena's heart raced a bit more rapidly. It was Marcie who breathed deeply and coolly as she observed the reactions of the other crewmembers.

"This is an answered prayer," Geena uttered, almost to herself.

A brief prayer by Dr. Monroe asking for success and safe returns echoed in the minds of everyone involved as the crew marched out in single file to the spacecraft. The full moon provided a luminous view of them in their uniforms, no doubt a sight that would have been the envy of any Hollywood producer.

The thrilling blast of the takeoff drowned out almost all of the cheers and applause from the grounds crew below. Moments seemed like hours before the vibration stopped. Then they heard, "All systems are go," as the next phase of their escape from the Earth's atmosphere was initiated. Shortly before the *Freedom Promise* reached orbit, the tank discarded into space. After a few minutes, they stabilized.

The four astronauts who were new to actual space flight—Captain Kelly, Marcie, Angela, and Geena—were experiencing a not-uncommon feeling of nausea and imbalance. Yet they countered this with deep breathing and anticipation that their equipment and training would help them. Soon these unsettling sensations subsided.

Once settled in, they had some time to think. Although the crew made extreme efforts to keep as much as possible secret, they knew that the mission, appropriately named Freedom Promise, had not gone undiscovered by much of the public. In efforts to keep as many details classified as possible, Mission Control had been more successful than others. NASA continued to deny rumors that prison inmates were involved, for example.

Geena wondered about her beloved grandmother in England and about her own life. *Will Nana ever even know about this mission?* She let her mind wander into a life that might have been. Realizing that most of her friends from school were married and had families, she wondered if such realities are in the cards for her. *How did all this happen? What's up with this?* Smiling to herself, at least she appreciated her own sense of humor.

They learned that Commander Harris Connelly was a veteran of two space missions and lived in Florida. The pilot, Sean McGraw, a native of Alabama and a seasoned test pilot of twelve years, experienced one previous space flight. Capt. Richard Kelly and the three women scientists were the rookies among the crew.

Angela thought of her lovable, precious Pop who guided her health, education, and spirituality. She valued all he taught, meant, and realized similarity of concern for her from her new friends and fellow crewmembers, Marcie and Geena. "Thank you, God," she uttered to herself.

Marcie knew her determinations to succeed throughout her life was built based on overcoming insecurities. She had learned to always keep trying and expecting the best of herself. She had wanted to tell her stepfather about this daring opportunity from the beginning. Although limited to what she could disclose, separate vetting of his background and his own experiences had permitted a bit more disclosure in his case. His conviction that she was dealt a great injustice by the legal system was at least partially addressed when he learned of the mission.

He constantly felt that the special circumstances, which led to her dangerous experiments, should have led to a lighter sentence. His testimony in her behalf concluded, by focusing on her motivation. "She was moved by a desperate attempt to save her mother. Her love for her mother and an overpowering desire to save another human being temporarily clouded her judgment." This modified insanity or diminished capacity plea was labeled as too little and too late by the prosecution. Although sympathetic to some of this, the judge agreed with the prosecutor.

Geena recalled Valentina Tereshkova, a former textile worker from the Soviet Union, who became the first woman to fly into space. Her forty-five revolutions around the Earth in just under seventy-one hours proved that women were capable of enduring spaceflight. *How things have changed since 1963*, Geena marveled.

Intricate insulation filled the interior of their craft, along with detailed wiring, flat-screen monitors, and specialized windows shielded, as necessary. As the newbies adjusted to their weightlessness and the seasoned astronauts too were acclimated to the craft, they prepared for their next tasks. Directing attention to the largest window ahead, Commander Connelly, remarked, "Look at that sensational view. Who could imagine?"

Angela, in particular, was awed to be so close to these sights, especially to the reflection of distant stars. She carefully identified binary and triple stars, indicating, "A binary star is a pair of stars that orbit each other." Explaining to Geena and Marcie, she continued, "Most of the multiple stars are too together and difficult to study as the lights blend." Able to identify one set of triple stars, she documented all her observations in her ever-present journal. Her "sisters in crime," as only they and only to themselves might address each other; also took extensive notes.

No one was idle; much was expected, and all knew Mission Control closely monitored them. Yet, not all was only somber. Their weightlessness continued as an exciting introduction to space. They had fun consuming water and food when floating. Constant amazement, produced by their window and views from other angles provided by the monitors inside the craft, was overwhelmingly breathtaking. Yet their constant consideration remained the seriousness of their mission. All led to their assignments on Europedus.

Angela recalled Captain Sterling's dictum, "Experienced astronauts are always prepared for the unexpected. Usual forces of weather, electron and other magnetic forces, and radiation can all create risk, sometimes deadly danger. The brave persons who go into space are to be commended for their courage, valor, and confidence."

———————

Two and a half days after the initial launch, the Freedom Promise reached its penultimate destination and prepared to land on the surface of Europedus. Commander Connelly provided clipped instruction about what each step was involved in the landing. Meanwhile, Geena could not control her composure as she thought about how unbelievable it is to land on the surface of a body in outer space. She almost whimpered, to the virtual delight of Angel and Marcie. "Look, she is human just like we are," Angela rambled to Marcie.

The seventy-six-ton spacecraft contained thirty tons of supplies and equipment, most of which would be left with the three women. Foodstuffs and potable water should last at least six months, after which, or before, another spacecraft was to return with additional supplies or with an assignment to return them if the mission was deemed successfully concluded.

The four male astronauts assisted the women in constructing living quarters and a laboratory. The allotted time considered was about fifteen days, relative to Earth days. Commander Connelly reminded them, "Space time is distorted by distance and the presence of material bodies, an effect we are used to as gravity. Little is confirmed about the climate, atmospheric qualities, or gravity on Europedus until further testing. This is one of your chief assignments." After the fifteen-day period, the men were to return in the *Freedom Promise* to Earth where they will prepare for future assignments. Mission Control had yet to determine who will return with supplies or potentially a third trip to retrieve the women.

Anxious to actually get started on the surface, each of the astronauts eagerly anticipated their orders. After external probes, determining temperatures and a related concern outside the spacecraft, Mission Control gave permission to proceed. The hatch opened to an odor much like old burnt cinders.

"Wow, this is something!" Captain Kelly declared. As test pilot and physician, his experiences and skills were deemed essential to the mission.

Commander Connelly replied, "Dick, this is my third mission, but it is just as thrilling as the first."

Sean McGraw, the pilot, and Tony James, the flight engineer, both agreed. Tony, a thirty-five-year-old civilian and a partner in the aeronautical firm, was responsible for designing and building the spacecraft. He was married and the father of two children. The pilot, Sean McGraw, at thirty-eight is a twelve-year veteran of the United States Air Force. He too was married, but they had no children, although he often spoke of his two Siamese cats.

Captain McGraw had piloted the shuttle under the direction of Commander Major Connelly, who was also thirty-eight and a test pilot in the United States Air Force. The women learned that Commander Connelly had never been married, although they thought of him as highly skilled and able, not to speak of being quite handsome. The mission crewmembers of the armed forces collected pay according to their rank. The civilian, Tony James, anticipated a healthy bonus for his firm and himself upon their successful return. An undisclosed, or probably not previously determined, amount of pay for the three women remained concealed.

All that is taking place mesmerized Angela, Geena, and Marcie. They could barely contain their excitement. "This is certainly something," Marcie declared.

"So true! It is indeed another world," added Angela.

"I'm sorry, girls, I just have to say it, it's out of this world." Again, Geena enjoyed her own play on words.

Commander Connelly led the group down to the surface, followed by the others. As all had left their space shuttle, they stood on what seemed to be an icy surface. Each insulated suit provided oxygen and removed carbon dioxide and moisture. Jet-propelled backpacks and specially molded shoes for protection and probable mobility completed their suits and helped ensure greater safety.

Reminded to be constantly vigilant, all were observing and becoming aware of all around them. This was for their safety and that of their fellow astronauts. Careful examinations and feedback helped with the authenticity of their discoveries. The women knew that the men were to return to Earth and leave them to continue in only, too short a time.

"We will have to get construction finished as quickly as possible," Commander Connelly instructed. "We want to leave these ladies as comfortable as possible." As he flashed a brief smile to them all, Marcie noticed a distinct wink, which could well have been aimed in her direction.

Unpacking began with the combined efforts of all seven. They retrieved and assembled the basics of a small lab, which was in the spacecraft's cargo area. To their amazement, the surface of the planet seemed to be more like that of Earth than previously believed. Even gravity seemed to be less, but proportionate, to that of Earth. This has made travel and construction easier than they expected.

The first few days seemingly going well as the small community molded together. The buildings, constructed on the top of the surface because of the hard rock, were coming together. Several water tanks, put safely into place, provided ample supply for drinking and bathing beyond their initial six months. They needed to soon determine if there was precipitation for continued water and if air quality was healthy and ample.

Well-insulated walls helped separate their living quarters for work, sleep, and hygiene. They were relatively happy with the safety and comfort their new home base provided. With her usual sense of humor, Geena turned to Commander Connelly, "Where are the curtains?" As she expected, he merely chuckled. By the end of two weeks together, the group had developed a great sense of rapport. They had actually enjoyed each other's company and developed a genuine friendship.

As they continued for several days past the expected fifteen-day prediction, all were pleased with the space home and laboratory the men had completed for the women. Major Connelly stayed in frequent contact with Mission Control and learned of intriguing news. Journalists, in major cities, speculating about their mission in diverse ways. Despite official and carefully worded news releases from Houston, it seemed as if everyone wanted to know more.

"What are they suggesting, and what is Houston saying?" Geena asked what is on all their minds.

"Houston is dancing around the details using high-tech space jargon. Everyone seems to realize it might not be a good idea for the public to know that over four hundred million in tax dollars is being invested on a mission that includes sending convicted felons into the unknown," Connelly answered in a teasing manner. "This would go against the grain of so many politicians of each political stripe, especially with current deficit and budgetary priorities. The current administration is already under scrutiny, and the general public seems to have a 'throw the rascals out' mind-set for all the incumbents."

"Some politicians have no sense of humor," Marcie declared as all laugh in shared agreement.

Major Connelly continued, "Fortunately, even among the political elite, only a select few know all the details of this mission. Fewer know about your respective incarcerations, but some word may have leaked out. Without confirmation, journalists will likely not publish any details, but the speculations among the tabloids may be another matter entirely."

As the time for the men's departure flew by, the women were confident but apprehensive.

"Are you really going to leave three defenseless women here? Do you expect us to work and explore without protection?" Marcie questioned as the men rolled their eyes.

"You three are *not* defenseless," Commander Connelly quickly declared, this time more boldly winking at Marcie.

During the last few hours together, Capt. Sean McGraw, to everyone's delight, surprised them all with a bottle of Dom Pérignon. His toast spoke volumes and the attitudes of all four men. "To the smartest, classiest ladies I have ever had the pleasure of traveling through space with, may God bless each of you with health and success and bring you home safely."

As they embraced good-byes, Harris Connelly kissed Marcie's cheek, yet as the men followed him into the spacecraft, her confidence wavered. "I can't believe they are leaving already," Marcie grumbled.

"Don't worry, Marcie, we will be just fine." The ever-adventurous Angela quickly replied, probably with more confidence than she felt. "We all have a lot to do, and time will pass only too quickly."

Seeking to augment this encouragement, Geena reminded them of how well prepared and confident their training had prepared them.

"I feel that way also," Marcie commented.

"I know we have a huge chance of success and survival," Angela predicted. "And hey, we don't have to drive the ship back."

As Mission Control directed the four men who had left, the women remembered them as their "protectors" sending good wishes their way. The *Freedom Promise* parted for its return to Earth. As the three women prayerfully bowed their heads, they requested a safe return for their newfound friends and for their own well-being and success.

When they could no longer see the departing spacecraft, the three women promptly entered their lab. Quickly reviewing the diverse equipment and supplies at their disposal, they were grateful for all the previous training they had undergone. Each knew that their primary goal was to acclimate themselves to a new environment. Dr. Jim had stressed how crucial adaptability must be. "Physiological and psychological challenges will no doubt take place. Even the relationships you have developed with each other may undergo significant change in this new stage of the mission." Initially, they had reviewed their plans to help one another in the event of emergencies. They relocated and reviewed medications and related supplies, to address.

In the absence of Commander Connelly, they communicated with Mission Control through a team of specialists in Houston. Jon Mattingly at the Lyndon Johnson Center was their primary contact. "You will stay in constant and regular contact with us, especially reporting all your scientific discoveries." His professionalism and the ease with which they were able to make contact with him had made the women feel more secure. Concluding with specific additional instruction, Mattingly signed off to let the women be with their busy assignments.

HOPES FOR A LOST SHIP

⟶⇒●⟵⟶

Twenty-three hours after Freedom Promise left Europedus, devastating news came to the three women. Mission Control should have been addressing them with the voice of Jon Mattingly. Instead, they heard a different familiar voice.

"Geena?" The voice from NASA was confident but a bit more emotional than usual as she recognized it to be that of Dr. James Monroe.

"Yes, Dr. Jim. What is it?"

"We have distressing news. Commander Connelly and the rest of the crew are in trouble as they orbit back to Earth. A dreaded but rare magnetic field with unstable electron particles has caused at least some damage to *Freedom Promise*."

"Oh no!" Geena's voice was almost strangled, her skin tightened around her face. "What are their chances?" Tears flow easily. These four men had become like family to her and the other two women.

Dr. Jim continued. "The crew is left about two hundred and fifty miles above the Earth's atmosphere in an abnormal zone. They are anxiously working to repair the damage."

"How bad is the spacecraft damaged?" She tried desperately to remain calm as Angela and Marcie, hearing only one side of the discussion, waited with barely repressed anxiety to find out what was happening. As she noticed this, Geena spoke, "Dr. Jim, I am going to put your voice on speaker so that we may all hear."

After waiting a moment, he continued. "A small erup-tion was discovered on the port side of the spacecraft during robotic inspection."

"Will they be able to repair it rapidly enough?" Marcie asked for all of them.

"We don't know how quickly they can make the repairs. To complicate that issue, the ship is on a course, if it continues to free-float, toward a further danger. An event horizon, the spheri-cal boundary of a black hole, is dangerously near them. We are praying that they regain control in time. They have to rewire some of access to their power sources and communication leads. It is essential for them to maintain contact with Mission Control, and selfishly, we need to know just what is going on. Yet these men are competent and capable. What we do know is that Major Connelly and his crew are methodically completing each task."

Marcie couldn't help but exclaim, "We understand they have the skills and training, but what about these new dangers, are they in any atmospheric or gravitational danger?"

One of the Mission Control scientists replied, "As you know, stratospheric temperature much depends upon distance and where the sun is at any specific time. They not only have to worry about magnetic fields and abnormal electrons. An even bigger concern is how the ship is drifting off course. The closer they drift off their current location, the hotter and more dangerous could be external and internal temperatures. That is likely the main danger."

"Dr. Jim, please keep us informed. We are devastated," Angela pleaded with a quavering voice.

"I know; which is why I wanted to be the one to break the news to you. I want each of you to stay busy. The best way for us to survive and succeed is to pray for their safety and stay focused. Try to concentrate as well as you can on the job at hand."

"We will try," they promised. "Thank you for letting us know."

"Ladies, I will be in touch."

"Thank you. We will be praying as well."

The *Baltimore Sun* headline typical, "Space Shuttle *Freedom Promise* Drifting miles above Earth's atmosphere while crew scampers to repair damage." Everyone heard the same general information repeatedly. Only the skimpiest of details had been made public; reporters, talking heads, and the general populace were anxious for additional information. Churches and individuals prayed for the safe return of the spacecraft and its astronauts.

On Europedus, the three women almost avoided each other's eyes and worked in eerie silence. After hearing the news, Marcie fondly recalled the warmth of Harris Connelly's tender kiss on her cheek before he boarded the spacecraft.

It was Geena, who in a firm but emotional voice asked, "Girls, what can we do to help this situation and not be paralyzed by anxiety and sorrow?"

Angela lowered herself to her knees and began to pray aloud. As the other two followed, they requested for protection, help, and safety for themselves as well as the four men on the *Freedom Promise*. They prayed for the immanence of God's presence and protection. Finally, they again prayed for themselves that they may focus on their required tasks and the rescue of the men aboard the endangered spacecraft.

———⊷⊶———

Geena was anxious to explore the area beyond their lab and living quarters.

Surprisingly the open air seemed pure and permitted them to breathe without a ventilated helmet supplying oxygen. Yet, they realized this could change as they traveled beyond immediate areas near their home base. As a precaution, they agreed to keep their helmets and oxygen within easy grasp.

The women all delighted in making new discoveries beyond what they had seen so far. Geena was especially anxious to investigate the possibility of plant organisms, although so far, rocky shale covered most of the land around them.

External temperatures in the area seemed colder but livable for them, with temperatures the equivalent of -5° Centigrade or 23° Fahrenheit. Geena began to determine relative weight and gravity in the area. Although less than that of Earth, the gravity permitted them to move about easily without worrying about needed weights on their feet or excess foot-pound effort used for travel.

"It is like an orchestrated visual spectacle, just needing musical accompaniment," Geena wrote in her journal as she contemplated the sky above with wondrous stars and light. Traveling some distance away, she was overtaken and delighted by the very beauty she saw. Realizing that she may have wandered further than she wanted to do at this particular time, she determined to head back to their base. Although she had an imprecise sense of exact direction, she was confident her advanced compass and other equipment would help her make it back safely.

Just as she retraced her steps, Geena glimpsed a shiny reflection, not too far, to what she thought of, as south. Upon a closer look, to her amazement, she saw a small rivulet, a stream of water. Anxious to relate this to the others, she took a moment to take a sample in a small vial she carried with her for such a possibility. Revealing this to her friends, they were all three excited to analyze the contents of the vial and relate their findings to Mission Control.

"The power system has been successfully repaired. However, the danger is not over until the repair to the damaged port side is completed and the ship deemed able to withstand reentry. We are optimistic that this will be soon and are preparing for a safe return."

The women heard this with cautious delight. "Thank you so much for letting us know," Angela responded for the other two. "We are all praying for their safety and success."

"We will provide more updates as soon as possible."

"Before you go, Geena has made an important discovery," Angela excitedly added.

"Great! Let me turn you over to your team consultant."

"Hello, Geena, this is Jon Mattingly. What have you found"?

"I have located a small stream of water about three kilometers or a mile and three quarters away from our home base. I didn't see its origin or any plant life. We are in the process of analyzing the water. We'll try to gain more information about its location and physical characteristics and provide details as soon as we can."

"Way to go, Geena!"

"Thanks! Take care of our guys in space and bring them home safe."

"We will, ladies, and I will relay those well wishes to them. Over and out."

After their scheduled meal and rest periods, they meditated upon on all they learned thus far.

During the next message to Jon Mattingly, Angela sent specific data they had garnered. "This small planet seems to not differ between day and night. There are so many luminous heavenly bodies from stars and other bodies to light up night as well as day."

Geena related her delight in the discovery that the water had no significant impurities and was safe to drink.

Jon was amazed at these discoveries, particular of pure air and water. "Geena, there is likely to be plant life you have been seeking."

"If it is here, we will find it."

"That's great. We'll be in touch."

The three women returned to inspect the newly found brook, especially on the alert for plant life and other unusual possibilities. They traveled in what they considered a southerly direction, careful to stay within about 1,500 feet of each other, examining every rock and larger stones on the surface and always staying within sight of one another. The lower gravity permitted quick movement as they covered quite a lot of territory quickly. Angela analyzed air and surface temperatures on an ongoing basis. She found the further south they traveled, the higher the temperatures seemed to read.

"This rocky terrain presents a huge variety of textures and geological types." Geena wrote in her journal. After quite some distance, they estimated about forty kilometers, or twenty-five miles, another and larger stream came into view. They took more samples for analysis and delighted by this new discovery. Deciding to use their jet-propelled backpacks, they planned to cover as much of the area as possible in that part of their exploration.

<hr />

Marcie, the most excitable of the three, shouted to the others, "I have found something. Hurry, quick! There may be life here!" She held in her hand what appeared to be a large dead bug about the size of a quarter. "I felt something hit my face, and before I thought, I smacked it with my glove."

Their enthusiasm abounded with each new discovery.

"This is wonderful, an astonishing find," Geena declared as Angela marveled. Each had renewed energy for any new discovery. Only too soon, the time allotted for the day's assignment to conclude was reached.

With no additional meaningful discoveries for the day, they trudged back to their tiny lab and forwarded their reports, including amazing photographs to Jon Mattingly. As he eagerly forwarded their reports on to others, all were captivated by their most recent success, centered so far on the appearance and dimension of the dead creature.

After their mandated rest, each of the women, excited by their discoveries, were anxious to get back to their explorations.

"These types of discovery—of vital information we now are already justifying the mission, don't you think, girls?" Angela asked the other two, who promptly agreed.

The next day, the three women were instructed to venture in a different direction; they are to take more time and focus. After donning their protective uniforms and helmets, they gathered their equipment and set out. The temperature was soon evidently more moderate. This impression soon confirmed by their thermometers.

This course led them more to what they considered, southeast. As they moved with care and determination, they were able to observe even more diversity among the crevices and rocks. Angela noted both the reddish-black to sepia-tone variety among the surface characteristics. After the relative thrill from the day before, the day is a trifle frustrating. "Aside from some rock and shale samples, nothing seemed to be rewarding their efforts."

Again, NASA defined rest periods, continued education and personal time for the women. Jon Mattingly's evaluation for the Mission Control specialists typical and positive. "Although each has distinctive personality and skill levels, they share commitment and diligence. All are successfully doing what we anticipated so far."

<hr/>

Although NASA and others had tried valiantly to keep details from publication and broadcast, soon some in the media blared, "There is a space vehicle in grave danger. Seven astronauts traveled on a secret mission. Now the remaining crew of four has been lost in space for ninety-six hours." In many ways, that raised more questions than it answered. Speculation intensified.

The bombardment of half news and speculation paralyzed the public. Dr. Jim's report to the three women on Europedus was succinct. "The craft drifted away from a safer area before the restoration of power was completed. This was determined after robotic repairs to the port side of the outer surface, that the raft should be able to stand reentry."

As the three women listened intently, Jon continued briefing, giving no false hope. "Gravitational levels and magnetic fluctuations will gradually intensify as the ship struggles to regain control. Our biggest fear is that of the black hole we discussed before. If the ship gets too close, it will disappear."

Angela explained to the others, "The temperature would rise to tens of millions of degrees." The possibility was horrifying to all three. They couldn't get past their anxiety of this possibility and, like millions of people on Earth, waited anxiously for updates.

The crew aboard the *Freedom Promise* fought to correct the navigation problems and head to Earth. Frantically, they strived to use every resource inside and outside the craft incorporated into its equipment. Officials at NASA, as well as everyone else, were reminded once again of the fragility of human life.

The silence for additional information was deafening. Thoughts and prayers continually poured out for the crew and their families. Dr. Jim led those at Mission Control in prayer. "We, as a nation under God, pray for the divine will of our Creator to bring the ship Freedom Promise and its crew safely back to Earth."

Hope dimmed when Houston officials again lost contact with the ill-fated spacecraft. The next few moments dragged at Mission Control. Must the nation face another mournful loss of distinguished crew? Finally, it was Jon Mattingly, who decided, "Let's wait a few minutes more before we give any sort of press release."

———⟶●◄———

Meanwhile, unbeknown to those on Earth, the spaceship's crewmembers, suddenly startled by a sudden movement, felt the ship angle and spring forward. As they experienced an incredible jolt, they were almost in shock. Gratefully, they began to feel that their streak of bad luck might be at an end. With this sudden movement, they had escaped the magnetic field, which kept them from being able to maneuver on their own. It was if the spiritual universe had sought approval and responded to the awareness and will of the Universal Father. Commander Harris Connelly and his crew were gratefully headed away from the dangerous path toward the gravitational field and the black hole.

Deafening cheers fooled the long-awaited message from *Freedom Promise*: "We're on course and headed home."

All at Mission Control breathed a sigh of relief with their renewed hope. Yet even amidst gratitude and relief, there was lingering concern. NASA officials were cautiously aware of the impending challenges of reentry to a damaged spaceship.

The concerns were gratefully relieved when just a few hours later, the *Freedom Promise* broke through the last levels of barrier and safely returned to Earth. The conical-shaped command module, which contained the remaining reentry equipment and living quarters for the astronauts, was the only portion of the spacecraft that returned to Earth safely. An assembly of anxious mission personnel, with a few vetted family members and well-wishers awaited the men's much anticipated arrival.

The women on Europedus celebrated in their own way, repeating words of scripture and singing "God Bless America." They were so grateful that the crew arrived back safely and pleased to have shared religious faith with each other. Extremely meaningful to them, was the broadcast comments from Major Connelly, who as an unashamed spiritual person, declared, "Truth is the domain of the spiritually privileged. We are so grateful, and especially that we know a supreme all-knowing and all powerful God."

The media's speculation and barrage of intensive investigation hadn't ended. Much was made of the fact that not all of the seven who left Earth aboard the *Freedom Promise* returned. Carefully scripted news releases strived to minimize details. The official reports continued to applaud the safe return of the spacecraft and its four astronauts.

WORLDS APART

All three women realized that living together around the clock and sharing experiences, ranging from seeking discoveries to even hoping another bug would hit one of them in the face, had given them all great insights. They had discovered each other's feelings, interests, ideas, and habits.

"We've not always agreed on everything, but have certainly learned to get along, to live in harmony. Probably because we respect each other," Marcie summarized. "We have become more than friends, more like a family."

Although, not any one of the women considered in charge of the other two, Angela and Marcie deferred to Geena in most instances. Jon Mattingly and the other Mission Control staff presented updates for all through her. Geena's and Jon's respect led to very good working relationships and a high-level rapport. In other ways, Marcie's medical background and personality had been almost a mother figure for the other two.

With the men returning on *Freedom Promise* safe, the women faced the next day's assignment with new confidence and excitement. They were directed to explore an area they considered west of their home base. Jon Mattingly's specific instructions were telling, "Use your equipment to measure levels of light and reflective characteristics as you search new areas. Always stay within sight of one another."

"Jon," Geena addressed him before they signed off, "The rocky terrain is more flat here that what we have encountered. Surface temperatures have risen to about five degrees Celsius or forty-one degrees Fahrenheit. Does that indicate a possible change?"

"It's a very good thing. It could well be season related. These warmer temperatures will make your assignments much more comfortable."

"Yes, right. I'm sure we'll be in cut-offs and skimpy tops soon."

"Now, Geena, just pretend you are all out for a peaceful, relaxing stroll."

"Thanks, I will pass that on. I'm sure Marcie and Angela will feel better," she concluded as they both laugh.

The ever-present light reflected on what seemed to be cosmic dust particles falling all around the women as they exited their laboratory. Angela, especially, was in awe. An opportunity to use their jet packs came as they encountered larger crevices on the service. Drifting above the surface, they searched and examined the area for anything of scientific value. Marcie's keen eye caught a glimpse of something shiny in the distance. That is more than just light, she decided. Before alerting Angela and Geena, she determined to investigate on her own. Speeding toward the reflection, she discovered a large spherical-shaped body of water, the largest they had encountered so far. Along the shore areas appeared clusters of what she was sure were heather-hued plants. The surface of the water appeared clear, except for some dusty particles on part of the lake and along some edges.

When she summoned the other two women, they all glared in astonishment. "This is amazing!" Angela and Geena exclaimed. They busily collected samples, checked the temperature of the rocky surface next to the lake and the water itself, and took many photographs. They were anxious to submit their samples to extensive laboratory examination.

As much as they would like to further explore the area, time was running out. They must return to their home base, transmit their discoveries, and wait for further instruction. Angela documented the specific location of the lake and reminded them that they must start back. Geena and Marcie headed back at a steady pace, not realizing that Angela had evidently decided to linger before following them. It was when they arrived back at their base they realized she was not with them.

"She was right behind us just a few moments ago," Marcie fretted.

"I know, Marcie. Don't worry. She will be along anytime now. She must have stopped to collect more samples," Geena encouraged.

Jon Mattingly was intrigued by the news and especially by the photographs of this large body of water and its plant life. "I will be in touch tomorrow. Get some rest. You'll need it for tomorrow's agenda."

"What do you think he meant?" Marcie quickly asked.

"I don't know," Geena replied, "but I'm more interested in locating Angela."

Despite knowing, it time for food and rest, Geena and Angela were both troubled by Angela's disappearance. Their pact of friendship and support declared unbreakable and took precedence. As the two women headed back toward the recently discovered lake, all they thought about was their missing comrade. Too much time had lapsed, and their fears had grown with that time. They vowed not to panic but realized how difficult it might be to keep that promise. They connected their arms as they shared a prayer, "Please God, let it be your will for our friend to be found alive and safe."

Keeping within sight of one another, they took slightly divergent courses to look for Angela. Soon Marcie uncovered her first clue. "Geena, her communication device is wedged under a fragment of rocks. Other large rocks in the area look as if they have recently fallen or otherwise been disturbed. There are skid-like markings on some sides. Her communication device must have been torn away from her protective uniform."

As Geena hurried to meet Marcie, she noticed something. "Look over there."

Finally, several yards away, they saw a stilled form, they confirmed it was their missing friend, but she was not moving.

"Hurry, Geena, she is pinned into a narrow section of crater."

They worked frantically to free her, anxious to confirm that she still alive. As if by the grace of God and in answer to their prayers, Angela's eyes flickered as they lifted her to safety. Marcie and Geena placed Angela on a flat rocky surface as Geena administered oxygen. In the comforting arms of her rescuers, Angela's limp body was carried further away from the crevice. Catching their breath and taking their time, Geena and Marcie proceeded swiftly, but with some difficulty, to take Angela back to the lab, thankfully without further incident. She had not responded any more as they travelled. Her vital signs were weak, and her breathing, shallow.

It seemed like an eternity and was actually many hours before Angela awakened and was alert enough to speak. "What do you remember?" both Geena and Marcie asked at once.

She answered with stammering difficulty, fear still obvious in her eyes and voice. "I saw something...mysterious...quite some distance away from where we'd gone today. It looked like the shadowy form of a human...or animal of some kind. Just as I tried to get closer...to make sure it wasn't an illusion...or my imagination, it disappeared as if running away...When I tried to follow, something hit me. I felt the air go out of me with no warning."

Realizing, it must be just imagination, Geena diverted Angela's attention. "Marcie found your communication device and is sure she can repair it. If not, we have a spare among our supplies."

"I can never thank you enough. Thank you both for coming after me."

"Get some rest. We'll talk more after much-needed rest and sleep. We can put everything in better perspective," Geena responded.

While watching over Angela the next few hours, the other two guarded her like older sisters. Her health and vital signs improved significantly.

Geena indicated that she had reported Angela's incident to Jon Mattingly. "We have some reason to believe we are about to find further reasons for our mission. Jon has hinted that we're to be informed of further assignments soon."

Marcie's observation was apt. "Geena and Angela, our purpose here isn't limited to what we have learned to do so far, is it?"

"I know, Marcie," Geena replied. "We might even say it's going to get even more complicated."

After several hours of well-deserved and needed rest, Jon prepared the women for a special video conference from the entire Mission Control at NASA. "Ladies, the secretary of defense has learned of a possible specific threat. He would like to address you himself."

"Oh no! Here it comes," Marcie muttered. Anxious to learn more, yet concerned about all it will mean, all three women listened intently. The secretary of defense spoke for almost two hours and let them know about a possible terrorism danger that goes beyond the Earth and beyond Europedus.

"We have known since 9/11 attacks how crucial it might be to protect our nation from potential danger, even including the possible building of defense systems outside our atmosphere. The wisdom of this, confirmed by a classified secret, is one I will share with you. There is a team of other human beings on the planet. We know it consists of two Russian cosmonauts and a rejected would-be astronaut from America, possibly others. They are striving to launch weapons of mass destruction from there to destroy parts of our nation, especially aimed at population centers and power grids. Most recently, we have intercepted messages from Europedus to strategic locations in Russia and the Middle East."

The three women could scarcely believe what they were hearing, striving not to reveal their feelings visually or in their voices.

"What do you expect us to do?" Geena asked, struggling to maintain a level of confidence and ability beyond what was actually there.

"I will explain," the secretary of defense promised. "In hindsight, we have underestimated this threat. We knew this might be possible but couldn't imagine it being this massive so soon."

The ramifications of this confession appalled Geena. "You people never planned for us to return to Earth," she coldly stated. She was unimpressed by the secretary of defense and his explanation so far. "You sent us here to spy on terrorists, to endanger us and much of what is going on upon the Earth, risking millions of people. And we are only three women!"

"Yes, Geena, we understand your anguish, but you are three extraordinary women with crucial skills and capabilities."

"Just what do you expect us to do?" Angela piped in.

"Angela, these men are known to be extremely intelligent. Do not underestimate them. We need you to continue exploring the planet. You are scientists' intent upon making your analysis. Work as comprehensively as possible from a scientific standpoint. Yes, we had not revealed all that we knew about who you might encounter. Yet, we are confident you can help us by striving to complete your research, at least as a logical cover for anything else you are to do. When you encounter them, as we know you will, be friendly and approving. Do not show any threat or belligerence. Other specific information will come later, and your assignments may be individually assigned."

"What are you saying, Mr. Secretary? Individually assigned for what specific purposes?" Marcie only thought of one reason to bring three women to encounter three men this far from Earth. "Are we pimping for the United States military or government?"

"Marcie, we expect you to gain their confidence by stressing that your mission is entirely scientific. However, keep your eyes and ears open, and let us know what you learn. We especially need to know about their equipment, but anything may be important. Let us know other details, what they wear, even down to what they eat. Be very careful, and realize that as nice as they may seem at some points, you may be assigned to exterminate some or all of them, as harsh as that may seem."

"I see. So you think that since we are all convicted felons, we are capable of murdering at your command?"

"Not at all, Geena. We respect what you all have achieved and what you are doing for your country. What has taken place in the past to lead to your respective incarcerations in each situation does not reflect psychological disturbances or mental imbalance. Extenuating circumstances exist for each of your convictions. On the other hand, what you have experienced and overcome has helped us appreciate your survival instincts and abilities, which are not typical of those who have undergone what the three of you have.

"We anticipate, and are confident, that all three of you will return to Earth alive and well. Our earlier declarations of potential restitution remain in place. We have just had to move up some of the things we might have expected you to encounter after spending more time on the planet. Future instructions will continue from Jon Mattingly and me. We are counting on you and have the utmost confidence in your abilities during this very delicate mission."

"Delicate mission, indeed," Marcie scoffed. "How logical is it for a government to send three women on a mission to commit murder?"

"What we are asking, as we addressed this issue before, is that you learn as much as possible. We constantly and carefully weigh all considerations provided by you and all of our other resources. It just seems appropriate to let you know that it may entail an assignment of final solution."

"Thank you, Mr. Secretary, for that inspiring vote of confidence." Geena couldn't help but comment with little tact.

Each filled with an eight-hundred gorilla in their thoughts, produced by that extensive briefing; the women were partially relieved that evidently their counterparts on the planet were not yet very close.

"Can you believe he considers us 'terrorist fighters' assigned to what he is calling a delicate mission?" As all laugh, each realized how much of an understatement, it no doubt was.

During the next several hours, their personalities reflected in their conversations. Marcie had given way to at least some public emotion and quietly cried at the same time. Geena resisted showing her true feelings by becoming belligerent. As has been typical, it was Angela who strived to keep them optimistic and composed.

"We have already accomplished so much, and I know we can do more. Yes, it is a lot to face, especially since we didn't expect this part, but we are in a position to help, if not indeed, save many others. We may possibly prevent a catastrophe," Angela remarked.

Uncharacteristically, Geena agreed. "You are right, Angela. We must do all we can to support each other. Perhaps we'll even think of ourselves as undercover space cops." Despite their deep concern, this brought giggles from all three.

Although the humor had helped, Marcie collected herself and acknowledged, "We must be grateful and positive about our own capabilities. This is not only about us anymore. Our feelings are less important than our success in this assignment."

Geena's humor again was typical. "Girls, this puts any specific study of a rock, molecule, or plant on the back burner."

In unison, they agreed as all refocused on their mission with a renewed commitment.

Without meaning to speak quite so forcefully, Marcie declared, "No one, nation or group, has the right to claim control of space. If there is a threat to Earth from Europedus or from another area in space, it is a concern of all nations and of humankind!"

"Yes, indeed, thank you, Marcie. That is true and profound," Geena noted as Angela smiled.

All three women concluded their preparations for the evening's rest with easygoing conversation.

—>•◦«—

Dr. Jon Mattingly quickly brought the next morning's briefing to the possibility of danger.

"We have pinpointed more specifically where the other humans are located. It is about 1,120 km or 700 mi from your location. The map we have prepared and are sending will provide details that are more specific. However, as you know, we cannot anticipate all potential obstacles or challenges. We rely upon you to be perceptive and aware of your surroundings. Be ready for an engagement with them at any time."

"What? We thought you had located them quite some distance away!" Angela quickly exclaimed.

"Yes, their command center is some distance away, but it is not possible to monitor individual positions as they move about, just as you three have done in your explorations and assignments, without jeopardizing your mission. Be prepared at all times for any distractions without warning.

"As you travel, you are to relay anything and everything to us, even that which may not seem to have much value at first. By the communications we have intercepted, these other humans are not aware that you are on Europedus. You will be a tremendous surprise. Be sure to maintain every appearance and perceivable activity of legitimate scientists' intent upon your explorations and research. Any notes are to be related to cosmology, biology, and related fields."

"Yes, we understand," they quickly agreed.

"Are there any questions?"

"What should we do if they see us?" Marcie asked.

"That is a very good question, Marcie. Remain extremely calm, make no sudden moves, and be just as surprised, as we know they will be, to see other humans. Use your poker faces or the animated versions of them. Be extremely cautious, especially on the initial approach. Do not, and I emphasize, do not display anything which could be considered a weapon."

Listening intently, they all complied. "After all, what else can we do now?"

"If there is nothing else, be prepared to leave in six hours. This will give you time to gather your equipment and supplies and get more rest. Memorize and destroy the map we have sent, leaving no evidence of outside planning. Stay together, and if you have any questions, I, or another member of our team, will be available round the clock. Good luck and God bless."

The next several hours required executing their instructions. They were cautioned to take only those necessary items for their survival and comfort and those that support their appearance as scientists. That included their data collection as they continued genuine scientific research. Their own basic academic curiosity and determination to continue the original assignment added to their efforts, which also helped authenticate their mission. Balancing mixed emotions of anxiety and curiosity, they headed out from their home base. After asking God for his divine guidance, their exit was marked by Marcie's asking about the possibility of running into other human creatures.

"Perhaps there will be 'little green men' from some planet world," she pondered aloud.

Geena's voice joined in with animated good humor, "You know what, girls? Nothing would surprise me now."

The outside temperature had risen to about 6° Centigrade or 43° Fahrenheit making it tolerably pleasant. The initial journey started smoothly with little surprises or threats, except for random but mild solar winds. Yet Geena, Angela, and Marcie moved painstakingly toward their objectives, constantly on the lookout for danger or randomness to what they had encountered so far. Their guidance equipment helped them maintain the appropriate direction. Other equipment had helped them monitor any possibility of motion beyond what they could see.

SUPPORT OF A MISSION

The Mission Control Center had welcomed the crew of the Freedom Promise who were responsible for taking the three women into space and helping establish a base for them on Europedus. All four men were supporters of Geena, Marcie and Angela; they had been keeping caring eyes on their efforts. At the center, they were delighted to learn more about what the women had accomplished since the men returned to Earth.

Commander Connelly was especially monitoring all phases of their assignment. He volunteered to head the mission to bring the women back to Earth when the time comes. All four of the men were pleased to note the astronauts' commitments to care for and assist each other, which reflected in the women's efforts as well as their own.

At least a partial relaxation of the classification standards imposed upon all family members and friends of all of the astronauts had taken place in the case of Dr. Andrew Adams, Marcie's stepfather. Marcie considered this special man who helped raise her as her own father. During the criminal investigations and prosecution of Marcie, he had been devastated. This seemed to have compounded his own frustration by the fact that he was unable to save his wife.

Dr. Adams found a friend and ally in Commander Connelly. He suspected Marcie to be aboard the crippled aircraft, which was somewhat reported by the media. Remembering Commander

Connelly, he recalled Marcie had mentioned his name as the person who would be at the controls of the mission. Dr. Adams and the commander had developed camaraderie, comfortably becoming supporters of one another. Dr. Adams had perceived that though dutifully obscured by professionalism, Commander Connelly also appeared to have more personal interest in Marcie, as suggested in a recent phone call.

"Dr. Adams. This is Harris. I just wanted you to know that all three of the women are in good health and are continuing to collect important information for us."

"Thank you so much, Harris. I have been worried about Marcie since losing her mother."

"As I was able to learn on our shared trip and information since, all three have established an exceptional rapport with one another. They are each bright, capable, and qualified to succeed. From the moment, we made the trip. I could tell they were also very protective of one another. Marcie especially caught my eye as a beautiful person with a wonderful personality and enormous compassion."

It was not what Harris said as much as the slight change in his voice when speaking of Marcie that prompted Dr. Adams to ask, "Harris, tell me. Do you have a family?"

"No, I never married. No doubt, I'm still looking for the right woman but haven't been doing so recently."

"When the ladies get back home, I would like for all of us to meet, especially Marcie, you, and myself. I believe you and Marcie could become good friends, and I am anxious to spend time with you as well."

⸻

Meanwhile at the NASA facility near Jacksonville, Florida, many of Angela's former co-workers continued to give her enormous support. Word slipped out to some of the media that a graduate from the Astronomy and Astrophysics Institute at the University of Chicago was among the three women who did not return from Europedus. Although striving to honor the government's request to keep things close to the vest, many of her former professors and other friends delighted by what they had learned about her mission. Most of them remained confident of her, despite the criminal trial and its results. The university consistently considered her a skilled scientist.

In London, Sylvia Belcher, Geena's grandmother, continued to pray for her safety and release from prison. She was oblivious to the specifics about Geena's more recent experiences, thinking that her only granddaughter remained in prison, wrongfully convicted of killing her abusive husband. Almost guiltily, Sylvia, who had a very strong dislike for him, considered it good riddance, but knew she could never declare that openly.

The seventy-eight year old widow continued to regret the great injustice, which had befallen upon Geena. She would have given her own life to have her granddaughter released. Since losing her parents at an early age, Geena's love and commitment was as unquestioned as Sylvia's love for her.

The three explorer's progress noticed and confirmed a change in temperatures. Their equipment registered fourteen degrees, or 57 degrees Fahrenheit. Angela's keen eye almost jubilantly noticed both a changed topography and increased existence of plant life; "Look, Marcie and Geena, how amazing the surface changed; from rocky stone, to glass-like lunar soil, to this new mixture."

Angela agreed, "It may well be because of the warmer temperatures." As usual, they took samples and continued the analyses.

Suddenly, Angela saw a strange figure in the distance. She stood motionless as the other two followed her lead. The figure did not seem to move at all.

"Is it a plant?"

"I don't know, Geena," exclaimed Marcie as Angela declared, "It looks like a rock formation."

Marcie attached a new, more powerful lens to her portable telescope for further examination. As they approached, thousands of reflective bright surfaces illuminated their area even more.

"It appears to be a waxy gray stone structure or figure, almost in human form," she informed them. As they moved closer, each had her attention focused on both the figure and whatever else might be around them.

"It almost looks like another pose by the model that inspired Rodin's THE THINKER." Angela commented.

It was very much like a human form carved from rock. Large and small chips surrounded the base. They gathered some of the chips for evaluation and study. It was about a meter and a quarter or five foot tall with an engraving at the base.

"This proves the existence of human life on this planet, whether from Earth or possibly from permanent dwellers here," Marcie enthusiastically exclaimed.

"My vote is not with the latter," Angela dryly noted. "That could well raise more questions than it would answers."

Translating the Latin inscription "Semper Paratus" for her counterparts, Angela reminded them that it is the motto of the United States Coast Guard. "It means 'Always prepared.'"

Looking closely at the base, they noticed what appeared to be initials carved at the side of the motto, reading "APK."

"What can that mean?" Geena asked.

"It's hard to say since we were not given names or bios of the humans or other creatures we suspect to be living here, thank goodness. Yet we can be grateful we were notified other humans from Earth are here," Marcie remarked.

Swiftly, they continued, following the directions indicated by the memorized map. Constantly vigilant, they observed anything that would lead to any encounter with other beings, human or otherwise.

Geena's reflections at least partially refocused on the sculpture. "Whoever APK is, he is not without talent."

Marcie nodded. Angela also agreed, adding, "The sculpture does not actually reveal his nationality, though."

"No, but the inscription sure makes it pretty obvious," Marcie interjected.

As time and anxiety had taken their toll, a bit of rare irritation was revealed between their interactions. As excited by their discoveries as they were, mounting concern and tension threatened to rob them of their focus.

Realizing this, Geena, in her motherly affectionate mode, gently reminded them, "Girls, we have got to settle down. We mustn't be unprepared or distracted when we encounter anyone. It is crucial for us to stay focused and be ready. Breathe deeply and concentrate, okay? Our attitudes will control our actions and results."

"You're right Geena," the others concurred.

As they traveled, attention returned to their discoveries. The lake and plant life were remarkable but upstaged by the amazing encounter with the sculpture and the many unanswered questions it helped present.

"This barren region is slowly turning into an ongoing oasis of surprises." Geena summarized her thoughts as they continued their course. Again, awareness and preparation for an inevitable encounter having never been far from their thoughts, each strived to balance preparedness and discovery for themselves and to empower each other.

LITTLE PEOPLE

———⟫●⟪———

Their adventure appeared to have become less stressful, at least briefly, as the three women accepted their new status. It was surprisingly different but true—the United States government had transformed them from felons to astronauts and then into government agents. What could be next, they each wondered. Seeking some semblance of what they do know, the three again shared some of their backgrounds.

Geena's wonderful experiences with her grandmother had helped her focus and become more determined to survive and succeed in all they were asked to do. The constantly optimistic Angela centered her mind on previous accomplishments and the work they had done so far, with this Europedus mission. "Whatever the final outcome, look at what we have been able to learn and do," she reminded them, along with herself.

On the other hand, Marcie focused on seeking forgiveness for having hurt others. She silently thanked God for the safety of the *Freedom Promise* crewmembers and asked for continued protective blessings for herself and the other two women. "Please God, let your will be done, yet, we trust it will bring safety and success."

Suddenly, Angela screamed a quick word of excitement. "Girls, look! There is something amazing ahead of us at eleven o'clock."

"What is it?" Geena urgently asked.

As she lowered high-powered scope lenses, Angela tried to reply. "It looks like a structure, like some kind of a tower. This may be a part of where the other humans from Earth have their base."

"Let's get closer, check it out and get some photographs," Geena suggested.

"That sounds like a plan," Marcie admitted, "but what happens if we are discovered? Maybe we should observe from a distance for a while."

All are in agreement as they proceeded cautiously, alert for sites that allowed them to approach closer but not easily seen. Crouching as low as possible near random rock formations, they checked out the exterior of a large, apparently human constructed, tower.

A relatively long wait gave them a chance to evaluate what had happened up to this point. All were positive and upbeat, pleased with their progress and findings. They were especially glad that they had all been able to get along so well and remain friends, making plans to keep in touch when they returned from their mission and back on Earth.

Beginning to resume their approach to the tower, Angela concentrated on detecting anything visually different while the other two followed her cautious lead. The three recalled with appreciation the warning by Jon Mattingly not to advance on any other explorers or their base of operation too early or remain in any one area too long. To be discovered, especially with cameras or other possibly incriminating equipment would be very dangerous.

"Let's watch the time. It's a long way back to our vacation condominium," Geena reminded them with a jesting reference to their home base.

These latest discoveries had infused them with adrenalin and speedier heartbeats. No doubt, this had helped them slough off fatigue. Reaching the lab in a surprisingly short time, they soon passed their discoveries and information on to Mission Control.

Jon Mattingly's final concerns both celebrated their success and helped assure their safety. "These photographs are wonderful. Be sure to delete your copies as well as anything else, which could be incriminating. That is very good work today, ladies!"

"What's on for tomorrow, Jon?" Geena questioned.

"We want all three of you to head out tomorrow and continue further. This has been a great start, but we need to know as much about everything as we can. Anything and everything you can learn, is our agenda."

"We have no guarantee that we will not be discovered or confronted, right, Jon?" Angela voiced.

"That is correct, Angela. That is why you must all be continuously prepared. Don't leave anything incriminating on your person or at the lab or private quarters. Not to put too much pressure on you, but millions are counting on your success, and the majority of them don't even know it. I continue to have faith in all three of you. Get some rest. I'll be back in touch in six hours," he concluded in a persuasive, encouraging tone.

⟶⦁⟵

Surprisingly, the women awakened to an even brighter "daytime" than they had experienced before.

"Jon," Geena excitedly reported, "it is as if we had our extremely bright day become even brighter. Is this a mirage?"

"No, Geena, the planet has gotten noticeably closer to the sun. This isn't really unusual, just something we couldn't expect or predict with precision. You may have this degree of brightness for several weeks or months at a time. It is probably best to anticipate some temperature changes as well."

The women listened as Jon elaborated on their specific assignments for the new day. "Proceed along the same initial course as yesterday. This time, be even more vigilant. It's becoming more and more likely that you will be observed and considered a threat."

"You don't pull any punches, do you, Jon?" Marcie spoke for all three as they listened with professional commitment.

"It is for your best interest. We want you to know and be aware of all we do. You are each an integral and important part of our team."

"I know, Jon, and we all appreciate you very much as well."

"By the way, ladies, check out the external temperature now. It should be more comfortable as you leave your condo."

Their bantering humor helped each become mentally prepared for their next assignment.

"The external temperature has warmed to a marvelous 19° Centigrade or 65° Fahrenheit," Marcie informed.

After additional, extensive briefings, they bade each other good-bye. As usual, Jon included a meaningful prayer, "God bless each of you and bring you home safely."

After a leisurely enjoyed breakfast of processed oatmeal, dried fruit, juice, and instant coffee, each of the three indulged in a soaking bath. The crew of *Freedom Promise* had helped rig up a bath that they usually use. However, they were pleased that the pure lake water nearby helped to invigorate them more than typical showers.

With the warmer temperature, it was a pleasure to don less heavy clothing. There was no change made in wearing the special form-fitting shoes and socks. They were pleased to relish in their discoveries of pure air, water, and warmer temperatures. These realities and being able to bathe made them feel wonderful.

Angela was especially delighted by the brightness of their day. "In the future, we'll be able to tell night from day, even though it doesn't appear so now."

"Angela, what would we do without your positive attitude?" Geena valued how often something, one or another of them had said, helped keep them motivated and on purpose. "Marcie, isn't she remarkable?"

"I think she would find a way to make us see the best in anything. You are so right about our Angela."

As they all laughed, it was a smooth transition to have a positive attitude as they got down to business at hand.

"We know what we have to do today. Let's get moving," Geena urged.

During their earlier rest, research specialists at NASA had poured over the forwarded photographs and specifications of the structure the women had encountered. This stone tower, as they had virtually all begun to think of it, was obviously the center of much attention and concern.

Jon had shared the consensus of scientific opinion that something was inside awaiting further movement or use.

"We believe this tower is crucially important to your tasks. Among other amazing things we notice, there are apparent openings, probably for ventilation. That they are large suggests something of a vast scale. Now we want you to move closer, measure and photograph all you can. If you can enter safely, do so. If confronted, be sure not to have notes visible—eat them if you have to." Not one of the women questioned his wise suggestions.

Several hours passed before they skillfully maneuvered themselves back to the tower. Angela kept a sharp lookout as Marcie and Geena measured, photographed, and inscribed notes. Entering the tower was more of a challenge than they expected; the entrance seemed to be firmly secure and blocked.

"Why would they obstruct and barricade the entrance if no one else is around?"

"I'm sure your guess is s good as ours, Angela. I'm not giving up that easily."

"We have come too far to give up now," Marcie agreed. "Let's look more closely."

Examining all surfaces with exquisite patience and care, they searched for any type of additional opening. It appeared as if there was none. Suddenly, they heard vibrating sounds that appeared to be coming from inside the tower. Silently, each reexamined the only possible entrance they had detected, which seemed securely blocked by overlapping plates of steel. As the women gazed fixedly on the steel, there became an increased volume to the continuous sounds from the structure.

It was not until Geena discovered a gap between the sheets of metal that they spoke to one another. She called to the other two, "Over here! I believe we have a small opening we can probably expand."

Angela and Marcie scrambled to peer through the opening partially blocked by Geena's obvious efforts to gain more access inside, complicated by her absolute amazement by what she had seen. Virtually dumbstruck almost ashen, the three strived to regain self-control and clear thinking. Inside appeared to be human, or at least human-like figures, but on a smaller scale, each dressed in snow-white jumpsuit like uniforms and moving about with eerie precision.

The women managed to regain some control, make mental and physical notes, and photograph their discovery. They counted twenty-three of the small figures. "This must be a dream or mirage," Marcie insisted. "This can't be real, can it?"

The diminutive figures were covered head to toe in their uniforms, wearing partial facemasks. They worked purposefully around very large machinery and seemed oblivious to the intruders. The noise from the machinery was only partially obscuring the sound of their precise steps and actions, yet provided some protection over the sound of the women's voices.

"They haven't seen us," Angela gratefully acknowledged.

"We have enough information to warrant returning and sending on to NASA," Geena determined. "Let's get out of here. It is crucial to send these notes and photos. We mustn't delay in destroying anything that would link back to us. Let's get back to the lab." Again fueled by excitement and purpose, they made short work of returning to their home base.

Jon Mattingly received their news with a mixture of delight and incredible disbelief. The photographs especially caught his admiration, but with concern that more questions were left unanswered by this new development. His directive was brief. "I want you to take extra precaution from now on. Stay where you are until I submit this to our Mission Control advisory panel of experts."

Their wait seemed interminable as the women awaited Jon's next communication.

"Why don't we put our time and memories to good work? Let's recall all of the details of what we experienced and saw today," Marcie suggested.

"Good thinking, Marcie," Geena quickly urged. "It may be that we can find important details that we have missed."

They began discussing their feelings of shock and disbelief, only later mentioning specific details. They helped one another to recall every aspect of uniform, mask, mobility of each figure and the equipment they were seemingly guarding or preparing in some way. "I remember that every little person's feet are covered in the same type of white almost luminescent outer wear."

"Yes, Marcie, I remember that as well. And their feet! Their feet seemed much larger in proportion to the rest of their bodies."

"I did notice an almost rhythm to their movements," Angela recalled. "There seemed to be absolutely no interaction with one another. Even though they moved and worked alongside one another, it was almost a mechanized routine for each. Yes, I did notice the feet seemed very large and the soles of their shoes appeared to be black or very dark."

"Good detail," Marcie exclaimed as the two of them looked at Angela approvingly.

They were discussing what kind of an ethnic group these almost human-appearing beings might have resembled when their long-awaited contact from Jon began.

"Ladies, I have just attended a crucial assembly by the powers that be about your discoveries. Your mission has escalated to top priority. A troopship to aid and assist you is to be underway within a few days. It is an intervention authorized at the highest level. Help is on the way. Obviously, it will still take some time for them to arrive. We have to consider an alternate plan. This includes the three of you."

"What can we do that will not jeopardize us or our mission even more?" Geena's determination to ask this without sounding alarmed was barely successful.

"Two of you are to expose yourselves to discovery. By that, I mean you are to more boldly approach the Tower. Take measures to encounter the other humans that we determined are already there. You know this is a dangerous phase of what we are asking of you. The safety of our nation and that of many others depends on your success. We have determined that the equipment you saw inside the tower is among the latest generations of what we only too loosely call weapons of mass destruction. Obviously, we need to deal with those and what they might enable."

"We are prepared to do all we can to be successful," Geena softly affirmed. "Give us a chance to do this."

"Mission Control decided to let the three of you determine which two are to go into the field and who is to remain at your base. It's your call."

"What do you think, girls? Does one of you have a preference?" Geena addressed her companions.

"No, I think we should draw straws," Angela proposed.

"Angela is right," Marcie concluded. "We are all competent and willing." Confident that what should happen, likely will, they ask God for guidance before drawing pebbles from a bucket. The smaller pebble determined who would stay at the lab.

Jon's typical patience was less than usual, as he asked, "Have you made your decision?"

"Yes, Angela and I will be traveling to the tower," Geena reported. "Marcie will stay behind to keep contact with you when needed and wait for us to relate."

"Prepare to leave at 0600 hours. Get plenty of rest. Be extremely observant and report all events to Marcie as often as you can. Your mission centers on this information sharing. We are confident and know you are capable. Go with God's blessing and our confidence that you will succeed."

All three women had difficulty sleeping that night. The evening and early efforts to sleep were filled with images of danger, anxiety, and challenges, crowding out all other thoughts. Morning came all too soon as the three women shared a substantial breakfast. Angela and Geena were to take provisions for the next thirty-six hours. They emotionally said goodbyes to Marcie, who wondered if she will see them again or if she herself, will be alive at their return.

MARCIE'S ENCOUNTER

—⇒⊃●⊂⇐—

"Yes, Jon, they left a few moments ago. We had serious discussions about how important this is and for them to succeed, but they left in good spirits."

"That's very good, Marcie. Don't feel as if we are abandoning you, though. I will be in touch throughout this, especially while they are away."

"I just want them to be safe. I want the world, our world on Earth, to be safe."

"I know, Marcie. We are all praying for that. By the way, Commander Connelly is just arriving. He's been very much a part of this entire mission and wants to speak to you."

With ill-concealed pleasure, Marcie noticed her breathing getting shallower and her heart almost missing a beat at the mention of Connelly's name.

"Marcie, keep your chin up! I've seen tremendous ability, courage, and determination in all of you. It shouldn't be long before I'll be helping bring all three of you back to Earth safely," Commander Connelly assured.

"It is so good to hear your voice, Harris. You gave us quite a scare on your trip back from here. Are you sure you want to undertake the risk of another trip to Europedus?"

"Of course, Marcie, I'm quite sure. I was in charge of taking you there and am determined to be the one making sure you get back safely."

Marcie's face glowed even more as they discussed his relationship with her stepdad, her father. For a few moments, she remained silent.

"Are you okay?" Commander Connelly asked.

"Harris, I am delighted that you have made contact with my dad. This is a wonderful, unexpected surprise."

"I'll tell you about it when we get together again," he continued.

The thought of being in contact with Harris Connelly, to any degree, gave her almost tangible excitement. An upward curve of her mouth revealed just a bit of her pleasure.

"I hope I can put a smile on your face, young lady," he concluded.

"You did. Thank you for caring!"

After her exchange with Commander Connelly, Jon cautioned Marcie about the possibilities that Angela and Geena may have encounters with nonhuman life forms, or aliens as it might be.

"Aliens, aliens, who cares about aliens?" Marcie joked with herself. Her actual concentration was on happier thoughts, especially focused on Harris Connelly. He was obviously a fine, upstanding professional. Perhaps a chief concern was whether he was only interested in Marcie and the others as a friend and fellow explorer on the mission or it could mean something more personal.

After her years of incarceration and self-incrimination, it was difficult to accept that someone might be interested in her for her own sake. Until the growing bonds of trust and friendship with the other women, she had begun to accept that she might have a life almost devoid of a close relationship. "At least some optimism and anticipation keeps growing," she muttered gratefully. "Whatever happens here, God has blessed me."

After the equivalent of twelve Earth hours since Geena and Angela left the base, Marcie finally received their report.

"We are estimated to be 160 km or 100 mi from our goal. A lot has happened, especially related to earthquake-like spasms and rockslides. The latter of these have been in all sizes and, at times, seemed not be stopping at all. For twenty minutes or more, we were unable to make any progress at all. Yet in between our two stopping periods, we did discover several areas of what seem to be distinct footprints, some partial, either human or very like human."

"How do you interpret the prints?" Marcie inquired.

"Marcie, they are about 15 cm or 6 in across and 33 cm or 13 in long, just a little larger than the average human male foot. There are at least eight prints distinct enough to measure. They are virtually identical. The sole imprint is plain without a noticeable arch and with subtle horizontal indents much like corduroy ribbing. We haven't taken photographs at this point because we don't want to risk being encountered by others with our cameras. If we are being observed as we expect, it's wiser to not endanger ourselves in that way."

"Thank you for the update. It's all very exciting. I'll pass this information on to Jon immediately. Please be extremely careful and get back to me as often as you can, and back here soon. I wish I could help you."

"Just knowing we can contact you and how much you care is enough right now, Marcie. That helps us tremendously," Angela responded.

"Before you continue this recreational hike, as Geena might call it, I have some news for you. Guess I'll steal her thunder of a little humor for a change. I spoke to Commander Connelly who was at Jon Mattingly's headquarters a while ago. He has volunteered to come after us when the time comes."

"If that time comes," Geena declared wryly.

"I believe that man has a particular interest in one of us, Geena, and I don't believe it is you or me," Angela quickly noted.

Although inwardly delighted at this thought Marcie was very thoughtful for a moment and then became evasive and changed the subject. "We will make it our business to succeed at this expedition and return home safely."

"Now that is the way to affirm what will be! Thank you for reminding us."

"Girls, please be careful," Marcie concluded. "Remember your best weapons are your brains."

A few less-severe earthquakes, having caused what appeared to be recently replaced rocks, continued to slow the process of Angela and Geena traveling at any great speed. They were exceptionally careful, especially when they encountered deep crevices or became separated from one another. Before long, they were standing within a view of a surprisingly fertile spot of land surface surrounded by the typical barren rock areas they had just experienced.

"Look," Angela cried out with surprise, "an oasis! I see areas of plants, water, and trees!"

As the two investigated, they discovered a cluster of trees with greenish-gray branches, which were almost feather-like. In the center of the trees was a pond the size of a small wading pool.

Geena muttered barely above a whisper, "I sure hope this isn't a mirage."

As they approached, they both touched the water to assure it wasn't an illusion. Reassured, they examined other details in the area to increasing delight. There they already felt more restful and relaxed, although they knew to exercise caution. After consuming their food and water rations, they took time to relax and rest. Some of that time delegated was spent on analysis, reflecting on what they had discovered before planning their next steps.

"We are enjoying our recreational hike, as Marcie put it," Geena reminded Angela, to the amusement of both women.

Angela and Geena awakened the next morning by the sound of marching feet. They saw what appeared as twelve smaller human forms, little people having clubfeet and swarthy white clothing. They were approaching the oasis. The women could do nothing but look in disbelief, their hearts pounding with amazement. Both were in sight of the creatures that seemed not to notice them.

The creatures carried large orange buckets, which they dipped into the water until each was almost full. In total silence, the women watched as the group, marched in single file back in the direction from which they came, carrying buckets. Only after the last of these was out of sight, Angela asked in total amazement, "Oh my goodness, Geena, what do you make of all that?"

"I don't know. They look like the same small forms or little people we saw at the tower. They seem to have eyes, but are they able to see? It sure doesn't seem that they can."

"I got a good look at the face of one of them. It looks a great deal like our own but is so swathed or wrapped you can't see much detail. Almost like an expressionless ghostly imitation of a human face. Their motions are completely different from ours. It's almost as if they are robotic or controlled by some type of programming."

As they reported this amazing news back to Marcie, she asked, "Did they speak to one another or make direct contact with each other?"

"No, and that's probably important," Angela answered. "Except for moving a virtually exact distance apart from each other, almost always in single file, they seemed to be unaware of one another." She went on and described details about their clothing, buckets, and behavior. "They all look identical, with no obvious gender distinction. They are all the same size."

Geena and Angela concluded their report to Marcie, and all wished each other the best. Each couldn't help but think of childhood stories of similar creatures as they followed them.

"We could be in an encounter which upstages Snow White and the Seven Dwarfs," Angela remarked. "Who, or what are they, where do they live, and what does it all mean for us?"

Geena dryly responded, "I believe we are about to answer at least some of those questions. Look ahead. Here are more."

The initial group from the pond had apparently returned to a larger group of the little creatures. Looking behind that group, the women saw in amazement that the little people were working, busy constructing what seemed to be simple, but effective buildings.

"They are working as we have seen them before. With no shared communication, much is being done in a brief time. We have reassurance that the little people still ignore us as if in their programmed efficiency," Angela quickly communicated these new observations to Marcie. "The buildings are made of stone and some kind of mortar. This is evidently from a large vat in the midst of their site and the water they retrieved helps them to stabilize their projects. Large rocks and stones are included from the abundant number we see everywhere. We are not close enough to see all the details, but the buildings are about eight feet apart and six feet high. There is a small entrance to each, which is covered by what looks like a shiny metal."

Geena paused for a breath and quickly continued, "The settlement almost looks like a group of semi squared igloos." Remaining at their considered distance for safety, both Angela and Geena memorized every detail of what they saw, especially the synchronized labor of the small creatures.

After contacting Jon and getting his feedback, Marcie's message was direct. "Jon wants you to move as soon as you can safely do so, back here. He isn't anxious but does not want you to remain there any longer than necessary, not to be in danger or uncertainty."

All three laughed. "This whole venture has been filled with danger and uncertainty. Is he trying comedy now?" Geena's usual sense of humor again helped prevail over their initial fears.

Back at the base, Marcie's emotions were only too wound up. The last many hours she had been on constant watch and concern, escalating her own concerns. Perhaps she needed an obviously earned break.

Angela and Geena were intently observant as they moved closer to the huts, examining them. "The rock is layered in some areas, much like gneiss, which is very dense and resistant to erosion," Angela remarked.

"What do you think of the buildings?"

"I don't know, Geena. In some ways, it's like a space version of structures on the prairie in the old west. They used whatever they could find. Some are sophisticated, like that first, one we call the tower. Others are more like stucco or rocks and primitive mortar. That mortar is amazing, though. It seems very resistant to corrosion."

"I don't see any further activity now that the little people have left the area. But dare we look inside?"

Both decided to first contact Marcie to update her and let her know of their plans. At first, Marcie's failure to respond not alarm either of them. "She's probably using the bathroom or conducting some kind of experiment away from the communication console." They decided.

With carefully chosen speed, the two descended to the narrow valley and began investigating the huts more closely. Four of the structures contained what appeared as articles of clothing, bedrolls, and other basic elements for a primitive tent or hut. The fifth structure was larger than the others. Inside, they saw two wooden desks laden with computers and journals. An impressive assembly of the latest satellite communication gear drew their focus. There, in the last hut, more of a storage area, virtually everything they saw in writing was in Russian.

Returning to the main rim above the valley, they regained some of their composure. Their shared excitement was tempered by ongoing concern for Marcie as they again failed to reach her.

"What has happened? Why doesn't she respond to us?" Angela demanded.

With great effort, Geena managed to conceal at least some of her concern, knowing she must be strong for her own sake and for Angela. "We have to keep going. We can't lose our courage. It's fine to be concerned, and Lord knows we want the best for Marcie, but we have to be optimistic. Let's take it on faith that Marcie is fine until we learn otherwise."

"Of course, you are right, Geena. I have to let myself lose my cool every now and then, I guess. It was just that time."

With at least some renewed confidence, both continued to concentrate on what they had discovered in the small huts and especially evidence of other humans having been there.

———◆———

As the group had earlier agreed, Marcie provided her true name and elaborated about her field of academic expertise.

"What about your other team members? Where are they?"

Breathing more regularly and noting that the man was apparently not carrying a weapon; she nonetheless realized this muscular man would have little difficulty taking care of himself if called to do so.

As if reading into what he thought of her lengthening pause before answering him, the man affirmed clearly, "Marcie, I have no intention of harming you or them. My name is Dawson Engels. I am addressed as Colonel Engels. I am a member of a special task force authorized and assigned to our mission by the Russian institute."

At this revelation, Marcie felt her face tighten in alarm. She barely audibly muttered, "I thought you were American."

"I am very much American. Authorized by Russia from where we left, we represent many nations who are cooperating for this important assignment. In a nutshell, we are to investigate and possibly confirm the existence of life forms beyond those we know on Earth."

Careful not to reveal her true feelings at this comment, Marcie realized she didn't believe him. *Now it's my turn to laugh,* she thought to herself.

Both were now extremely cautious about revealing more information to the other. "How many others are in your task force?" Marcie questioned.

"There are twelve: six Russians, two Frenchmen, two British, a Canadian, and one American. That would be me."

"Where are you based on this planet and how long have you been here?"

"Marcie, you ask entirely too many questions for someone who doesn't seem to want to give out much information herself. However, I'll let you know that we have been here two months and have a camp a few hundred miles from here, toward what is north for those of us used to Earth directions. Now what is your story? I can tell that you are American."

Striving not to reveal her suspicions, Marcie continued, "As I said, my team members and I have been searching geological formation, flora, and possibly fauna here. The other two are out gathering specimens now. We have been here since May and report our findings and analyses on a regular basis."

"Well now, it is going to be interesting for me to report, 'By the way, there is an attractive female scientist, and possibly there are more, here on this godforsaken planet."

"Colonel," Marcie interrupted with quiet intensity, "we had better hope and pray that God has not forsaken this planet, or us."

"True, I stand corrected," he carefully acknowledged and proceeded with carefully chosen phraseology. "On this unproductive, at least so far, area many, many miles from Earth and seems to be an utter desert. By the way, since there seem to be only two of us within any measureable distance, you might consider addressing me as Dawson."

Marcie was a little ambivalent. Secretly impressed by his eloquence, she was anxious to report the interchange to Jon Mattingly. In addition, she became increasingly anxious about what the other girls were doing, wondering if they were trying to contact her.

Colonel Engels seemed in absolutely no hurry to leave. After a bit of reflection, Marcie asked, "Dawson, how did I end up right here?"

"I arrived at your quarters when you were leaving. Perhaps you were startled and fainted, so I carried you here as a precaution until I could learn more about how to help you. You are actually not far from your base. I'll take you back safely and soon, now that we know you're okay."

Barely concealing her alarm, Marcie couldn't help but tell herself that Engels must be the American they were pursuing. Was he indeed a dangerous criminal? "Please, Dawson, just point me in the right direction."

"Marcie, I brought you here, and now that I see you are not some kind of alien ready to attack me or endanger yourself, I insist upon delivering you back."

Striving to control her imagination, Marcie agreed to let him escort her. *After all, what can I do if his plan is to exterminate me?* As they reached her lab, Marcie's feelings were quite mixed. Not wanting Dawson to examine their work and living area, she was still more comfortable being back at their base.

"Marcie, I know it must have been a huge shock to see another person here, especially without any warning. I know it sure was for me." After a brief pause, Engels continued with obvious concern. "I want to check your blood pressure and pulse before I leave. Do you want me to stay until your friends return? If not, you may want to give them a heads up before I reappear."

With her concerns alleviated, at least for the time being, by his obvious compassion, she agreed and allowed him to follow her into the lab.

"This is quite a set up you have here." He adeptly checked her blood pressure, examined her eyes, pulse, all with a deft touch. A signal from his communication device interrupted their interaction before he bade her farewell with a promise to return.

Mulling over what had taken place; Marcie reputably tried to contact Geena and Angela. Finally, she heard Geena's voice, "What is going on? We have been trying to reach you."

"Geena and Angela, I've had a visitor." Both listened intently as Marcie explained her last few hours and what had happened.

Angela succinctly asked, "You mean we are out looking for the bad guy and the bad guy finds you?"

"You could put it that way, but he let me know quite a bit. I learned that he claims to be one of twelve who are on a task force from Russia assigned to discover the possibility of aliens."

"Marcie, try to contact Jon immediately. We want his approval to return to you."

"I will, and then let you know. Are there any developments you want me to relate to him?"

The two explorers briefly related their discoveries for communication to Mattingly, especially referring to the stone structures and settlements.

<hr />

The communication Marcie had with Jon Mattingly at Mission Control brought more startling surprises.

"Marcie, I'm sorry it was such a shock for you to run into Colonel Engels. Perhaps we should have prepared you more.

"What are you saying, Jon? You knew about him?"

"We recently were made privy to the Russian Space Institute's plans, including the assignment for this group to help counter the bad guys. It isn't uncommon for Russia to keep details of this sort of mission very close to the vest."

"What about Engels, the American?"

"Colonel Dawson Engels is retired United States military officer. He is actually our informant, in case the Russians didn't want to be cooperative. We wanted to get him assigned to such a group but weren't sure if we were successful until recently. We are fortunate that this time, the Russians were cooperative. We should have told you sooner but have wanted to wait until determining their location. It looks like you helped do that for us. Russian intelligence officers learned through their informants of serious threats to governmental, military, and industrial centers here on Earth. Colonel Engels and his group are actually on our side."

"Are you telling me that they are not here for the sole purpose of looking for nonhuman life forms or aliens?"

"Tell me, Marcie, what did you think of the colonel? Was he believable?"

"Not even close. I thought for sure he was one of the three we are here to seduce."

"Oh no! Now we're back to that idea, are we?"

After thinking it over for a moment, Marcie admitted, "It is comforting to know we have allies. What is our next move?"

"Have the other women return to your base. It is important to update all of you and prepare for a meeting with the colonel and his group soon. Marcie, are you able to contact him and his group?"

"Not directly, Jon. I'm sure he will be in contact with us soon but can't be sure when. He left rather abruptly but did promise to return."

"Be careful, Marcie," Jon concluded with his typical warmth and goodwill for all of them.

"We will. Thanks for caring, Jon."

UNFRIENDLY NEIGHBORS

———◦◦◦———

It seemed forever before Marcie's long awaited reunion with Angela and Geena became especially satisfying. The three "sorority" sisters met after a long separation. Angela and Geena began to realize how energizing it was to be back with Marcie and to the environment, of which the three of them have become adapted.

After a planned rest, a video conference call between Jon and the three women began. The interchange included bringing all up-to-date on discoveries and plans for further instruction. Ultimately, the women were to coordinate their efforts with those of Colonel Engels and his team. Specifically, the women were to become involved in minimized danger from the bad guys, now that they know the colonel and his team are allies.

"Jon, when will we come face-to-face with this colonel and his band of space hoods?" Angela asked.

Since it was only Marcie who had encountered Engels thus far, Angela and Geena were determined to permit a more levity to alleviate their anxiety at this stage. No doubt, Angela had imagined a parallel of the group with Robin Hood and his merry men.

"Angela, I assure you it will not be long. I advise you not to refer to them as 'hoods.' They are competent professionals just as you are, and they deserve respect." His clipped tone was more reprimanding than usual.

"Sorry! My tongue gets in my way every now and then. I didn't mean that literally," she quickly apologized.

"Okay, now. Get back to me when you have made contact with Colonel Engels. We will then get them involved and prepare to finalize our plans."

"Thanks, Jon." Angela's voice was more appreciative and in appropriately contrite agreement as they concluded their conference.

Preparing for a well-deserved rest, the three women bantered with one another and asked more probing questions at the same time.

"What did you think of Colonel Engels, Marcie?" Geena asked.

"Yes, Marcie. Inquiring minds want to know," Angela added.

"Well, that is an excellent question. Although he and I were both very careful, I found him to be intelligent, gentle, and kind. He was inquisitive, but so was I. Both of us were reluctant to trust one another."

Angela giggled. "Hmm, was he handsome, fit?"

With a grin, Marcie rejoined, "Could it be that we have been away from civilization long enough for a man to be appealing or tempting?"

All replied with grins and affirmations.

"Go on, Marcie, what about his looks?"

"Colonel Engels has dark, almost sun-kissed, skin and eyes which are very alert, obviously missing nothing. He looks to be extremely fit and muscular. His face is rugged with strong features. If I hadn't been so suspicious, my overall impression would note he is handsome and kind."

"I don't know about the two of you, but I think I am in love," Angela responded to Marcie's description as all three chuckled.

The three women awakened the next morning to an unfamiliar sound, much like that of a car horn.

"Hello there. Is anyone up yet? I've come for breakfast."

Marcie was secretly pleased to recognize the voice of Col. Dawson Engels and swiftly went out to greet her new acquaintance.

"Colonel Engels, we have been expecting your visit. Please join us."

"Remember, Marcie, I asked you to address me as Dawson, and I would prefer your lovely companions do the same." Glancing to the unusually silent Angela and Geena, he entered their quarters.

All three women noticed how trim and fit he is.

After a brief moment, Engels offered, "I may well be dreaming. It has been my experience that most female scientists are rather plain, dumpy, or otherwise unattractive. All three of you are certainly exceptions."

Angela quickly decided that Marcie's earlier description had not done him justice. Geena looked at Angela in silent admonition to behave, at least at first, in what she was prone to say aloud. After simple introductions, the four spent time elaborating on their backgrounds, academic specialties, and related matters before focusing on their mission that NASA and Mission Control had assigned them. Very soon, time had flown by, and it was time for their next video conference.

Jon Mattingly's summary was both succinct and significant, as it involved the three women. "You are to share all of your observations, discoveries and concerns with Colonel Engels and his crew. Colonel, I know you will be most cooperative as well. These three women are trained and professional."

"Dr. Mattingly, I'm confident that is the case and will certainly help aid and protect them as well."

"Good. They will brief you on what they have learned. Although they don't know details of your mission, it is fortuitous that it coordinates with what these three women are to do. I am pleased you and your team are available. Thank you."

During the next few hours, Geena prepared, as instructed, to lead Colonel Engels to where she and Angela encountered the little people and to the structures, which seemed likely to house destructive weapons.

"Colonel, are you ready?" she asked.

"Yes, Geena, I am ready. But it's fine for you to call me Dawson if you like."

Engels was in high spirits and quite prepared to accompany Geena, while Angela and Marcie had instructions to remain at the lab. There, they were to forward any relevant communication from Engels or Geena to NASA.

The two quickly departed, aided by luminous starry lights above them. Geena silently thought how wonderful a setting this might be under circumstances that were more romantic. As if having read her thoughts, Dawson mentioned, "It is a beautiful, picturesque sight."

Approaching the first structure that Angela and Geena had encountered before, clouds had created more darkness than they experienced in the first part of their travel. Engels and Geena carefully paced themselves a short distance from the tower. At his request, Geena crouched closely behind Dawson. Almost painfully slow, they gradually walked closer to the structure with painstaking caution.

"Do you see or hear anything?" Geena didn't realize she could whisper that quietly as she hoped he would do the same.

He nodded, indicating the slightly ajar entrance to the tower. "We need to get closer, but I can already see something disturbing. Who could imagine so much weaponry here, and much of it I don't recognize."

"The sound must be what we thought were generators before, but they are actually louder now."

Pointing to the largest machine inside the building, Engels replied, "The loudest sound is coming from that particular machine. It seems to be converting mechanical energy into electrical and the reverse of that process, almost in a continuous loop of availability. I'm sure it's main purpose is to keep all the equipment at a constant temperature."

With scarcely concealed irritation, she thought; *He supposes I don't know what a generator does.* However, the greater priority of their goal prompted her to refocus.

Engels quickly, but thoroughly, examined as much of the equipment and weaponry as he could while Geena photographed everything. Only too soon, they determined it was best to leave rather than remain and risk discovery. They managed to return to a rocky outcropping nearby, giving them some shelter. If anyone is to see them, it would be more difficult there, than at the tower.

Feeling safer from this distance, the two looked at one another with a little awed concern. Both provided a clear and organized report back to Angela and Marcie, who forwarded to Mattingly at Mission Control.

As they awaited feedback from their report, Engels and Geena took a breather and rested, not sure just how much time would lapse before they heard back from Angela and Marcie's forwarded message to Jon Mattingly.

Geena finally broke the ice with only a half-serious question. "What do you do when you aren't chasing felons?"

"Actually, I am a retired American military from the special services. I had my twenty years in while I was young. I suppose, I got bored with doing nothing. In a nutshell, my other team members and I were recruited to apply our skills and do exactly here what you, more or less, have learned. I jumped at the chance to lead the group on this mission. Don't forget, Geena, we're on your side; Yours, Marcie's, and Angela's. Like you, we didn't know the details when we began. Imagine how nice it was for us to discover three stunning women here, respectable and respected scientists, no doubt, but still beautiful.

"The Russian government's space institute has constant cooperative agreements with NASA. The Russian and United States governments have shared interests here. Ours is an international team intent on avoiding a grave danger. The Russian intelligence agency has learned of a probable threat by renegade former space experts and mysterious powers that be that are behind them. We are striving to learn as much as we can and prevent a worldly disaster from taking place."

"I think I understand. You are the equivalent of Dirty Harry sent here for unconventional warfare, right?"

They both laughed. When he asked for her background and after consideration, she was about to explain her imprisonment, they were interrupted by the sounds of marching feet.

Soon, they saw the same little people, or some very much like the ones the women had seen before. They unwaveringly headed toward the tower. In astonishment, the colonel's jaw dropped.

Almost with a grin, Geena remarked, "I take it you have not been introduced to the little ones."

"I had no idea. Sure, I listened to you but could only imagine from your description just what you saw. This is amazing."

Engels and Geena noticed that the little ones were marching in very precise pairs. "This group total is twenty-four," she told him. "Dawson, they don't seem to be aware of us or even to one another. They seem robotic with fixed eyes and almost programmed uniformity of movement. What do you make of them?"

"I want to get a closer look. You stay here, but I need to get closer and see what we can learn."

With mixed feelings, Geena watched as Colonel Engels stopped right in front of the last pair of little people. With mounting concern, she whispered, "Oh my god!"

Almost, as if miraculously, the two smaller creatures stepped around him as if he were an obstacle they were supposed to avoid. Marching in step quickly, they returned to their formation. An anxious Geena greeted him as he returned to her side. They shared their wonderment before regaining their composure and prepared to contact Marcie and Angela.

The colonel's long experience handling public relations had honed his communication skills as was evident in the professional dictated report to Mission Control. "The little people appear oblivious to the presence of human beings. They are aware of us or anyone else as merely an obstruction in their environment. We are in little danger at present, even if in their vicinity or entering the tower."

Geena was as impressed by his professionalism and obvious courage as she was troubled by his boldness. Yet she listened in approval even while thinking, *Is he for real? Are we really going to be in the tower with those strange little people? He does seem more and more in command and quite able to accomplish all he intends to.*

Almost before she could process her thoughts, this became their assignment as determined by Mission Control. They were to enter the tower, analyze all they see, including the activities of the little people. Engels and Geena carefully entered through the opening. Just as Engels predicted, the little people showed no awareness of this intrusion.

Back at their lab, Angela and Marcie anxiously awaited news from either Engels or Geena. Marcie instinctively reassured Angela that very effort helped both of them as Marcie believed her own assurance that all would be fine.

"You are a good friend, Marcie. You always know just what to say and when."

"God has given us healthy minds and an abiding faith. We can resist our fears! I know that he places us where he wants us to be."

Both shared a few moments of silent prayer and then concluded by reciting the Lord's Prayer together.

———

Back in the tower, Geena watched Engels approach one of the virtually identical little people, slowly but purposely. He reached out to offer a handshake just as Geena thought her heart would stop. Her breath slowly returned to a more complete contraction and expansion as the colonel's gesture was ignored.

Engels glanced at her as he muttered, "Unfriendly little cuss!"

Geena rolled her eyes as she watched to see what Engels would do next.

Refocused upon the interior of the building, they both examined rather routine hard rocky surfaces. The walls appeared to be igneous, relatively uneven blocks with unusual sealing mortar, as the women had seen before. The twenty-four small creatures were moving about in single file. They seemed to be smoothing rough surfaces around the equipment, cleaning or doing tasks related to maintenance. Each completely focused on a particular task.

Engels remarked to Geena, "They are like regular little dwarfs right out of Snow White."

As Geena wandered to the left, inside the tower, she discovered a partially hidden door. It was easy to miss, but she found it concealed by two panels of sheet metal that didn't align completely. When Engels pushed the panels apart, they both entered the room carefully.

A desk and other equipment dominated the dim interior of this space. Using powerful flashlights, they saw computer reports, Russian ledgers, and similar data alongside portions of fuselages and rocket parts. As they examined more closely, Engels immediately recognized a container for power boosters and combustion accelerators. "They have quite an arsenal here," he barely got that said before they heard human voices outside the building.

Geena's mouth became extremely dry, and she barely breathed. She and Engels dowsed their lights and quickly crouched down as far from the desk as they were able to do so. Barely breathing, they listened as the voices got louder.

Geena almost gasped as powerful beams of light shone into the room. She and Engels remained silent as the beams disappeared and the voices became quieter. Fortunately, for them, the "speakers" were just giving everything a cursory check.

Colonel Engels quickly scanned the interior of the larger space as he extended his hand for Geena to follow. "Our characters from Snow White are gone. Were you able to see the faces of the other two?" he asked.

"Are you kidding? I was terrified and had trouble focusing on anything specific," Geena exclaimed.

"That's understandable. If found discovering anything in here, it could have been severe. I'm grateful they didn't notice us or that the barricade was pulled away. I do wish I was more knowledgeable in Russian. I couldn't catch most of what they were saying." Remarkably, Geena didn't respond.

On their return, both were relieved to put distance between them and the tower. Pondering upon the weapons and other equipment they had seen, Engels was so deep in thought he missed Geena's first few efforts to get his attention. Finally, he noticed as she raised her voice.

"Dawson!"

"Yes, Geena, what is it?"

"I thought you might want to know what they were saying."

He asked in barely hidden amazement, "You speak Russian?"

"I became fluent in Russian several years ago while studying in Minsk and then Moscow." She began to playfully repeating much of what they had heard, yet still in Russian.

"Okay, you have convinced me, and I am very impressed. But now, English, please."

Without gloating, she efficiently began to summarize. "They were talking about the little people we saw, calling them KEBOWS. They are using some sort of magnetic or physiological mind control powered by present and residual light. Evidently, these KEBOWS are only able to see or directed by certain kinds or levels of light intensity. They mentioned it is getting close to the time they will need to reprogram their 'little friends,' as they called them."

"Wow! What do you make of it?"

"It could be related to the brightness of light or a certain spectrum of light. I'm not sure. From what I gathered, these

KEBOWS might have their degree of obedience changed by alteration in light they experience. No doubt, the KEBOWS are native inhabitants of this planet. In some way or another, individuals from Earth have gained control over them."

"Did they mention anything else about others, who might be with them, or did they mention names at all?"

"Yes! One called the other Nicolai. He was the more vocal of the two and was excited about annihilating large areas of the United States, especially large metropolitan areas. I was unable to catch the name of the other one, but he sounded American. I have to tell you, though—these are both very scary men. They expressed to have little regard for the human race, no matter what nationality. Nikolai is especially livid that the Russian government has mistreated him in some way.

"The other, seeming to have an American speaking accent, was in total agreement. The two of them seemed to feed off each other in opposing any rational rules from any country. What I don't understand is how they could become accepted for any sort of space mission. Who is behind them and under what pretense are they authorized to be here? They had to have extensive help in getting here."

"Yes, quite expensive help," Engels confirmed, deep in his own thoughts. "What else did you learn?"

"Not a lot, but they were in a hurry to report to someone at their command post, who is presumably named Ivan. I took it that this Ivan must be the one in charge. This was likely a routine inspection of the tower before they were to return to Ivan and to whoever is with Ivan. They didn't appear to have urgency, at least, not right now. Nikolai reminded the other man how important their mission is and how crucial it is to succeed. The information we have is disturbingly significant. Let's get this information back to Angela and Marcie so we can forward to Mission Control."

Retracing their steps back toward the women's lab, they were suddenly interrupted by an authoritative command in English, "Halt!"

"It seems like forever since we have heard from Geena and the colonel. I'm getting anxious."

"Me too, Angela. Nevertheless, they must be fine. There has been no distress signal or anything like our backup notification."

"I hope you are right. Jon is scheduled to contact us very soon. No doubt, he will be concerned as well."

"Ladies, give me an update. Have you heard anything?"

"Jon, the good news is there is no bad news, not yet anyway."

"Thanks, Angela. I just trust there isn't a problem other than them not having been able to send a message."

"Marcie, you seem especially quiet."

"Jon, it is just that we feel so helpless. It is dispiriting sitting here and waiting to hear anything. It is as if we are stand-ins for a play, not being able to perform our craft or do our part."

"The two of you indeed are doing your part. You are supporting your comrades right now by your positive thoughts and prayers while waiting to hear from them."

"Then as Shakespeare so eloquently put it, 'Why does my blood thus muster to my heart?'" Marcie questions.

"Just be positive and optimistic. Keep alert for their sake as well as your own."

"Jon, if I might interrupt, I understand what Marcie means. We're concerned but we've had lots of time to wait and become anxious. We are imagining all kinds of things that might have happened. The unpredictable is always predictable in our minds," Angela explained.

"Ladies, I understand but want to remind you that fear, is not the best response. The old idea of positive thinking has a great basis in truth."

"If you could give us something positive and active to do, no doubt that would help. We'd feel better, and it would give us more of a sense of accomplishment," Angela proposed.

"Angela, you are right, and I'm sure Jon will agree," Marcie interposed.

"That is true. Give me a few moments. I am just the guy to help out with that."

Inspired by Jon's confident reply, the two women planned to give assiduous attention to the suggestion he made, but a gnawing feeling still existed as they had already been thorough in their analysis. Yes, he assigned them to look again at their discoveries.

"Jon, you have a talent for intrigue. However, we have examined and reexamined every rock, plant, and water sample within reach," Marcie almost reluctantly countered.

"Marcie, what we haven't found yet, we don't know."

"Jon, what kind of hogwash is that?"

All laughed at this quick rhetorical question, but Angela and Marcie were aware and appreciative of Jon's efforts to boost their confidence and alleviate their anxiety.

"Okay! On a more serious note, doing nothing is not the answer. We are much better off being busy. That will help our mission as well," Angela acknowledged.

"That's true. I understand," Jon quickly offered. His firm and consistent optimism was just what the women needed, particularly since they respected his expertise and had learned to appreciate his caring personality for them and the mission.

"First, there is nothing the two of you, or we at Mission Control can do to rescue your comrades if they are in danger. I'm not being cruel, it is a fact. You must remain optimistic, no matter how grim things may seem right now. Second, it is crucial that we all stay focused. This will help in many ways. Third, do not lose your sense of worth. If you believe you aren't important or have become expendable, it lessens your effectiveness and makes you less likely to survive. You are important to yourselves and to one another. Moreover, with what we are learning now, you may well be important for humans all over the planet Earth. The United States population is generally unaware of your sacrifices and efforts to assure their very survival.

"I am forwarding recent data to you from our National Security Force, which will help get you up-to-date on what we know about the inhabitants of Europedus. Through our Russian counterparts, we have learned that the creatures you describe as the "little people" are indeed indigenous to that planet. Cosmonauts discovered them many years ago, but this fact was kept classified by order of the Soviet, the Russian Scientific Intelligence Agency, and various levels of their government. That scientific body learned how to program these native creatures to be submissive and follow commands almost like a robot. In effect, they are virtually obedient slaves to whoever controls their programming."

"What you are telling us is that religious cults may exist in space!" Angela and Marcie exchanged disbelieving glances as Jon continued.

"Yes, there are significant parallels, but some interesting differences. Those you encountered have been isolated from their female counterparts as an element of this controlling mechanism. You will learn more about this from the data I'm forwarding. What I think would be helpful now is to study this information thoroughly and get to know as much as possible about these creatures before you see them again. This will enhance your likelihood of communicating with them, given that opportunity."

Marcie's next question revealed more than casual concern. "What exactly is this Russian agency, this RSIA? Who are they, and are any of them here now? If so, how many?"

"All the information you need is included in this ensuing transmission. Study all of these details and prepare for our next briefing via this video-conference program. We will discuss your further questions and go from there." After their farewells, Jon added his wishes and prayers for them.

Both Angela and Marcie couldn't help but reflect mutual longing for a more normal world and a place for them within it.

"No! Not this time," Marcie reminded Angela not to be negative or depressed. "Maybe Jon's little pep talk is just what we need after all. Why don't we take a little excursion and see what lies ahead?" Breathing deeply and with determination, both equipped themselves to prepare for what they, tongue in cheek, referred to as another field trip.

THE PRISONER

———⟫●⟪———

Geena and the Colonel had had a lot going on, and not in a positive way. Almost without thinking, they heard a human voice with a familiar command to halt. Both stopped in their tracks and stood motionless and silent, barely letting themselves breathe. Finally, the outline of a male figure emerged from outside their sight and stopped about ten feet right in front of them. He was clad in yellow space combat fatigues and held a weapon of some sort in his gloved right hand.

Geena was the first to speak. "Are you American?"

However, the shadowy figure only stared at her while slowly moving closer.

The two noticed his left arm seemed to be reaching toward some sort of gear on his back while he steadily held the weapon aimed at them. Colonel Engels figured he was possibly reaching for a more lethal weapon and determined he must act quickly. Pointing to something above and behind the figure's head, Engels yelled for his attention. As the stranger's glance veered off them for a split second toward where the colonel distracted his attention, Engels lunged forward. Within moments, Engels overpowered their would-be captor and seized the weapon and gear pack. Both Geena and Engels appreciated this drastic change of control.

Eager to abandon this immediate area, Geena and Engels quickly secured their prisoner with restraints. Contacting their lab, Geena was almost breathless but delighted to contact Angela.

"It's about time we heard from you two! Thank the good Lord. We were afraid something terrifying had happened."

"We're okay. Just a lot has happened. We're on our way back now and bringing a prisoner."

"A prisoner?"

"Yes! I can't really say very much about him because he hasn't spoken a word since giving us a command to halt. But it was in English. He caught us by surprise and pulled a weapon on us. The good news is the colonel overpowered him and now we are on our way back."

"Good, we'll meet you."

Marcie and Angela started their return to base.

"Well, that was a short field trip," Angela said with little disappointment.

The two of them were anxious to see for themselves that Geena and Engels were safe and in sound shape. In addition, they were extremely curious about this mysterious prisoner.

"What are we going to do with a prisoner?"

"I don't know, I guess we'll have to put our heads together and think about this one, Angela. Can you imagine a jail in space?" They stared at each other in silence. Meanwhile, Engels led the way ahead of Geena and the effectively controlled prisoner.

"Are you okay, Geena? Am I moving too fast?"

"No, not for me, I'm not sure about our speechless friend, though."

As the prisoner stumbled along, he seemed distressed and dazed by his misfortune.

———➤◆◄———

Before long, they reached the lab, now referred to as Command Center B. Angela and Marcie greeted them with delight, but the excitement of the disheveled prisoner became upstaged by news transported to their communication console.

From Interpol, via NASA, they learned that "there is a ring of hired assassins who plan to kidnap the president of the United States and his family." From Jon's elaboration, they discovered that this plot was suspected as directly linked to space terrorists on Europedus. Until the threat, and all it might entail, and thoroughly analyzed and dealt with by homeland security, little else seemed important.

Interpol's methods and motives were above reproach. As a nonpolitical international peace-keeping agency, its function is to help each country to deal with transgressors effectively. Particularly concerned with international crimes, they assist in sharing knowledge and helping justice departments of many nations deal with criminals while operating under the laws of each country's sovereignty.

To safeguard the privacy of further conversation, Colonel Engels escorted the prisoner to one of the water towers. There, he firmly fastened the man with handcuffs and a locked chain.

NASA continued its briefing and relayed orders to the colonel. All three women were much more assured than before and grateful of Engel's obvious leadership skills. After the conclusion of the conference call, they waited for his comments.

"Ladies, "he began, "our mission has stepped up a notch. We must gather all the information we can from this prisoner and any others we might encounter as well as the data they have forwarded. NASA wants me to head up our next steps but to limit the involvement with the three of you whenever possible. That's not to keep you out of the loop as much as to minimize danger. There are definite things we all need to do. We'll start by interrogating our prisoner. Geena, it's obvious we may need your skills in the language department. He may understand Russian."

"Sure! How do we start?"

"First, I want to offer him some food and water. We don't want him to think we are barbaric," Angela quickly offered.

"You are absolutely right, Angela. I will stand guard if you will volunteer to take him something to eat. It may be that your sweet smile will help loosen his tongue."

"That Colonel Engels has such a way with words and he is always protective, a true gentleman." Geena quickly noted as she winked at Angela.

Shortly afterwards, Marcie and Geena watched as Angela and Engels returned from their assignment.

"What happened? Did he say anything? Could you understand him?" Marcie inquired.

"Not anything I could understand. At one point, he seemed to mumble, but not in my direction, as he ate the food. I asked directly what is he called, but he didn't respond to that. He just drank some water and hung his head. He did take his glove off to hold the water. I thought we might try to lift some fingerprints."

"Good job, Angela. I probably wouldn't have thought of that," Marcie admitted.

"Okay, we'll give him a little more time to himself before Geena tries to speak to him in Russian," Colonel Engels quietly suggested to them. "We need to share our observations and determine who will take the next step. Who of the three of you should try to engage a chance meeting with the other humans here?"

"Colonel, are you asking for volunteers?" Geena asked.

"Geena, yes, I guess I am."

Marcie expressed what she'd been mulling over, "I believe these other humans, villains or not, would be less intimidated by women on first encounter. I volunteer."

"I agree," added Geena. "Since my Russian may well help, I want to go with her."

"Good. If we agree, Angela will remain at the lab as a primary contact for the two of you as well as for my team. I'm working on a schedule for the two of you to contact the probable enemy forces and for us to stay close behind."

—➤●◀—

As they approached the water tower, the colonel asked, "Geena, if you will please, speak to the prisoner."

She obeyed with short, clear questions. Everyone waited anxiously for any response. The man finally looked into her pale blue eyes with an intense, virtually unblinking stare. Determined to gain enough trust or respect for some response, Geena tried again. With a brief repetition in English of what she was asking in Russian, she pleaded, "Please tell me your name."

After what seemed forever, he gradually changed his mood. Speaking in broken English with a heavy Russian accent, he replied, "I am Karl, Karl Romanov." His dark eyes seemed somewhat less severe as his facial muscles began to appear more relaxed.

As he continued replying to Geena, there was a mixture of English with Russian phrases, as if he did not know the appropriate idioms in English.

"What do you want with me?" Karl asked.

Not willing to give a direct reply, Geena responded by asking him why he had halted them with an armed weapon.

"I was startled to see other people, other humans here, so far from Earth." His clipped, evasive answer was without elaboration.

Asking about the little people in white, they had encountered, Geena listened, "They are space aliens, not humans from Earth. We call them KEBOWS."

Confident that what he was saying was at least partly true, she continued. "What is their purpose?"

"They are building a new community in which they are to live."

"Who controls them? With whom do they communicate?" Continuing similar questions to little response, she took another route, "How many are in your group of astronauts? Are you here on an exploratory expedition of some sort?"

"I am here with several international scientists. We are planning to build space station here. We want to purify world."

Reading between the lines, Geena determined a more sinister true goal. They clearly wanted to purify themselves and destroy the world. Had they not heard Jon Mattingly's warning, this encounter with Karl Romanov might have taken another direction in her judgment. She then understood the threat this man and his group were to the world. Satisfied that he was not ready to divulge any further information, Geena left him alone for the immediate future. She carefully concealed her abhorrence toward him while returning to the lab.

Bombarded by questions from the other women and Colonel Engels, Geena efficiently began, "He explained to me that the little people, whom they call KEBOWS, are somewhat brainwashed or programmed. They have been, at least temporarily, overpowered by energy, hypnosis, or something. He defined KEBOWS, the name given them by the Russians, as Kremlin Ethnos Band of Warriors. He is Russian and understands some English. I did learn his name, or at least the one he gave me.

"That is about everything of any significance, except that he claims they didn't know we were here as well. We sent copies of the fingerprints from his drinking container to NASA. They will forward them on to Interpol for identification."

Colonel Dawson praised Geena before he prepared to return to his base and brief his men. "I will take our prisoner back with me. We will set up some kind of secure lockup. Perhaps he'll be impressed enough to become more informative. Don't worry, we won't result to torture, but we do want to know that we mean business. He might try to get more comfortable here with you kind, pretty ladies."

"Aw, shucks, Colonel. You are going to make us blush!" Geena gestured.

Jon Mattingly soon contacted them with news from the fingerprint examination. "Your new friend has been identified by Interpol. His name is confirmed as Karl Romanov. He is a former Russian cosmonaut ousted by the Russian Space Agency for endangering his fellow crewmembers. During a space mission in 2001, he drank too much vodka while in command of his ship. Even his fellow cosmonauts accused him of reckless behavior. Since then, a motley group of terrorists, primarily Russian and other areas of the former Soviet Union, have enlisted him because of his background. As we come up with more information, we'll let you know."

"Thanks, Jon," Marcie acknowledged. "Colonel Engels is on his way with Karl to his base. He will no doubt bring you up to date himself, but the plan is for Geena and me to take the initial approach in locating our target with Engels and his men nearby."

"Please be careful, Marcie. Our prayers are with all of you. By the way, someone by the name of Commander Connelly wishes to speak to you. Okay?"

The smooth relaxed tone had an immediate effect upon her. "Hey, Marcie, how are you?" Commander Connelly greeted.

"Hi handsome! It's so good to hear from you."

Jon pretended not to eavesdrop as the two revealed more than a passing interest. They continued to chat for a few minutes before saying farewell. Both Geena and Angela joined a lasting hug as Marcie shared, "His last words were, 'Take care. We have a date sometime soon.'"

Trying to be patient, all three anxiously awaited hearing from Colonel Engels. After almost twenty-four hours had elapsed since Engels and Karl left, Angela unnecessarily reminded them, "I hope nothing has happened to the Colonel"

"I doubt if Karl is a threat to the colonel," Marcie reassured them.

"That is so true. Our good friend has proven he can take care of himself. He'll be just fine."

All three women strived to ignore their anxieties and focus on the affirmatives. They realized their assignment was important for themselves and for the occupants of Earth.

Before long, Colonel Engels returned to them with an impressive group of others. Except for one or two who remained at their base to guard their prisoner, there were nine or ten men. The three women were quietly in awe of their appearance, each outfitted in dashing, impressive uniforms. All were fit and equipped with weaponry.

Introductions were brief, exchanging glances with approving nods. Yet they were professionally purposeful. The three women discreetly, but more directly, glanced at one another with approval. All knew that each of the merged group had duties that took priority.

"I have briefed my team on the basics of our plan, mapping out how we are to begin, and contingencies for further instruction. Marcie and Geena, you will head out and seek to make contact with the Russian group. Our men will follow in two discreet groups with a short time and space in between. When Marcie and Geena have reached the area where we think they'll make contact, we'll have reinforcements close." He directed instructions to the two women. "Be sure to continue your roles as trained scientists with only peaceful intentions. Keep your eyes and ears open. Be very careful what you say and do. Are there any questions?"

Glancing to Marcie, Angela raised her hand, "I do have a question. What about the prisoner, Karl? Did he divulge anything else? What did you learn from him? Who is guarding him?"

"Let's just say the prisoner was very cooperative. We gave him some vodka, food, and shelter. He's becoming increasingly cooperative, even providing a diagram and further information about the people with whom he is working and where they are based here." Looking at Marcie and Geena, he continued, "I'll go over further details as we are in route."

Marcie and Geena expressed their farewells to Angela, who stood bravely alone, almost in unnatural attention. Only too soon, the small army of hopeful defenders disappeared beneath the brilliant sky.

ALONE

———⟨⟩———

Gratefully comforted by reflections on what they had accomplished, Angela recalled the excitement of the take-off, the wonderful images of Earth from the spacecraft, and the thrill of their perfect landing. "How can it be that five busy months have already flown by?" she mused. She was especially grateful for the NASA crew who took them to Europedus and their own final assurance of safety after so many dangerous threats.

She was grateful for the love of a wonderful man who saw something special in her and selflessly fulfilled the role of her caretaker and benefactor, a further ministry to what he had consistently done before. "He made me a member of a loving family, even though often it was just he and I," she acknowledged. "I give thanks every day for him and for my wonderful new friends here. God, I am ready to accept your plans for me. Thank you for all of my many blessings. Amen."

Angela dutifully contacted Jon at NASA headquarters, reporting the others' departure. "Jon, I wish you could have seen them. The sight of that group leaving here gave a new meaning to 'dirty dozen.' They were reverent, professional, attired smartly and efficiently. Colonel Engels is extremely organized, a masterful leader."

"That is good to hear, Angela. What about you? Are you having a letdown about now?"

"You know, Jon, I did for a moment there. But by the grace of God, now I'm doing just fine. I'm optimistically prepared for whatever comes next. That being said, I'll be constantly in touch and will appreciate any feedback from you, the other women, or the Colonel."

"Good girl, Angela. Yes, I'll personally be directly available to you anytime while you are alone there."

After Jon's farewell, Angela busied herself, especially in updating her journal. She included precise details of everything of note since Colonel Engels led the prisoner, Karl, away. She thought to herself; *I wonder just what kind of persuasion the colonel and his crew used to get Karl so agreeable. No surprise there was at least some vodka involved.*

The hours seemed like weeks before any further contact, this time by Marcie.   "Angela, we have separated from the colonel and his team. They are intentionally several hundred yards behind us. Geena and I are within sight of what looks like a fortified camp. There appear to be six igloo-shaped stone buildings, much as we've seen before. Each is about the size of a two-car garage, with the exception of one, which is larger. The only visible activity so far, has been from a group of the little people, or KEBOW, as we have learned to call them. There is some sort of unusual flag with red stars and yellow circles flying from the front of the larger building. The KEBOW all seem to be busy tidying up the outside area."

"Thanks for the update, Marcie. It is so good to hear anything from you. Please, do be careful."

"We will. Don't become alarmed if you don't hear from us often. We'll try to keep in touch as regularly as we can."

Angela recorded this conversation in the base log as well as on her own journal before reporting to Mission Control.

———⟫●⟪———

Geena and Marcie had little time to reflect on anything except the matters at hand. Thankful that the backup team headed by Colonel Engels was near, they, nonetheless, realized how much danger was possible. It was at a pace almost painfully slow that they approached the KEBOWS. Yet the KEBOWS continued their activities without obvious reaction to the women, again, almost in a programmed or hypnotic trance. No other living creatures seemed to be anywhere.

Geena cautiously approached the largest structure and, after a brief glance, motioned Marcie to her side. The other area Marcie had been inspecting was most likely sleeping quarters. The two entered the larger building where they saw a number of desks with computer monitors and other recognizable equipment. Large projected screens identified the skylines of New York, Washington, DC, and Dallas, Texas. One area seemed to picture the gold vault at Fort Knox, Kentucky.

Immediately, Marcie whispered into her transmitter, informing Colonel Engels and his team what they had learned. His response was cut short by the sound of voices approaching the building entrance.

"Colonel..." Marcie began to stammer," I need to get back to you."

With a voice of concern and accustomed command, he quickly asked, "Marcie, what is happening?" His transmitter went completely silent.

Geena and Marcie both knew they couldn't risk caught inside this building. Looking about, they saw a small opening in the wall opposite the entrance. No doubt, it had been initially included in the structure for ventilation. It took a great deal of determination and effort for them to squirm through the narrow opening and exit the building. As quietly as they could, they left the area, and soon encountered the colonel and his group to everyone's relief.

"Thank God, you found that opening," Engels concluded after noting how dangerous it would have been caught inside. Discovered studying their plans would have been drastic.

Engels directed them to return to the compound but to approach from the direction farthest from the larger structure. "Before you get too close, make certain they hear you. Remember to look astonished to see other humans."

Although, pleased with this plan, Geena prevented herself from commenting by his precise instructions.

"I want the two of you to relax, loosen up. Take a deep breath and then start purposefully toward the compound," Engels concluded.

As planned, it didn't take long for Marcie and Geena to be discovered. Two large figures turned in their direction, shouted with alarm, and virtually tackled them. Suddenly everything went blank.

Not sure of just how much time had lapsed, Marcie awakened lying on her back in total darkness. She rubbed her eyes and tried to gain enough saliva to speak. "Geena, can you hear me?" There was no response.

Marcie gingerly climbed to her unsteady feet and began a tentative examination of her surroundings. Feeling along a firm, chilly wall, she determined it was part of an empty room. Roughly twelve by twelve feet, it's very plainness brought concern. Finally, she felt a rough area of the surface, possibly a hinged panel near the floor. Yet, what can she do?

Almost with surprise, Marcie remembered and removed a small knife, concealed in her shoe lining. Striving to carefully, quietly pry at the hinges, she tried not to become frustrated at her confinement. In the darkness and quiet, she listened for any sounds in the area. Mustering extra determination with each jab, she quietly rejoiced as the metal latch gave way, only to catch again, with only a few inches opening gained.

Marcie froze, wondering if anyone had heard the sounds. The small opening had allowed some light, and she thought hope in her imprisonment. "Where is Geena? Have they hurt her or even killed her?"

At the base of another wall, she discovered small grates in the side. The wooden frame looked more fragile than any other part of the walls. Furiously picking away at the frame, she managed to gain more light, much like a door slightly ajar. After what seemed like hours, the edge of the grate fell away to reveal her possible escape route.

Marcie fought her own fears. "Will I even fit through this opening?" With no time to spare, she removed some of her bulkier clothing and mentally measured her size against the jagged opening. She shoved her clothes through and struggled to follow. Since being on Europedus, the girls had had some bone loss but kept fit through extensive exercise. This turned out to actually benefit Marcie in her effort to escape.

Marcie squirmed, scraping part of her skin while forcing herself against splintered wood and metal obstacles. Fighting excruciating pain and apprehension she might be stuck, it was a blessed relief to push once more and fall through the opening. Ignoring bleeding hips and legs, she grabbed her clothing and scrambled to a nearby clump of brush. Redressing her shivering body more completely, the compound, she surveyed, showed several much larger huts from the one from which she escaped.

Cautiously looking about the area, she quickly receded further into the brush. Marcie caught a glimpse of Geena as two uniformed humans were sternly leading her. "Thank God she's alive," Marcie uttered under her breath.

Geena remained quiet when two of her captors began speaking in Russian, giving no indication that she actually understood what they were saying. They dragged her to one of the huts located away from the largest building, and as instructed, in English,

Geena entered the hut. They secured the opening, and the two men then purposefully walked away toward the other huts.

Compelling herself to wait after the men disappeared out of sight, Marcie finally emerged from her hiding place and raced to the hut where Geena was confined. Lifting the locked plank had required more effort than she had expected.

"Geena, are you okay? I was afraid they had killed you. Hurry, let's get you out of here before they come back."

"Marcie! Thank God you found me!" Geena exclaimed.

Geena followed Marcie to the clump of brush where she had been hiding. The two crouched down together and began to update one another.

"What happened? What have you found out?" Marcie asked. But before Geena answered, Marcie looked at Geena's glazed eyes. "I think we have both been drugged," she avowed.

"Marcie, those two men spoke Russian. They were discussing how long they would have to wait for me to come around so that they could interrogate me. They know I am American and are sending for someone they refer to as Capo, much like the term of a mafia boss in the States. This is likely a nickname for him. I don't know if they speak English because when I would ask about you, all they did was look blank and shrug their shoulders. I thought it best not to let them know I understood Russian, at least for the time being.

"One of the men, called Nikolai, is the one we encountered before. He is very aggressive and angrily rough. The other one that Nikolai called Ivan seemed at least somewhat more compassionate, but it could be like the good-cop-bad-cop ploy. Marcie, I think what we have to do is this: put me back in confinement before they return. The best way we can gain more information is for me to talk to this Capo."

"As much as my instincts tell me for us both to run, you are right."

"Two, we have nowhere to run."

"Right again. Do you know where our backpacks are?"

"Yes, I saw them thrown into that building just to the right of the largest building. I will try to find our radio transmitters if I can."

Within moments, Marcie left Geena locked up again and quickly searched the smaller building for their belongings. Returning quickly, Marcie quietly asked, "Geena, are you going to be all right in there?"

"Yes. There is a cot. I'm warm enough, and they have left water and rations."

"Good. I found our backpacks. I am taking mine with me. I'm also taking your radio but have left the rest of your things. That way, if they discover my escape, they'll think I have abandoned you, not knowing where you might be. I will let them capture me again after I give feedback to Colonel Engels."

"Great. Keep focused. Good luck, Marcie."

Returning to her sheltered spot within the brush, she hastily contacted Engels. He was surprised but pleased that she had retrieved her radio. Calmly, Marcie described all they had encountered and experienced. She paid particular attention to the comments of Ivan, Nikolai, and the mention of the one referred to as Capo.

"Are either of you hurt? Did they use force?" Engels questioned.

"The only force I am aware of is some sort of stun gun or something like that. It could have been chemical gas perhaps. I awakened on a hard stone floor inside a small very dark building." She continued describing the building's size, her experience with the hinged panel, grated grill, and delight in finally exiting. "Squirming through the grate was painful, but well worth finding Geena."

"I want you to go back to the village or whatever they are calling that settlement and find out all you can. Then resume contact with me so we can know how to advance."

"They don't realize that Geena understands Russian, at least not yet."

"Good. That's a plus for now. Take her radio back to her since they don't know you have either. If they discover and attempt to confiscate them, try to convince them that you need them for safety, either health, communication, or whatever it takes. We will not initiate contact with you unless necessary but will be close by. When it becomes imperative to infiltrate the camp, we will. Find out everything possible about them and their plans."

⟫◆⟪

Nikolai's voice rose to high-decibel rage by the discovery of the broken grate. He unlatched the entrance where they had left the prisoner. Capo and Ivan joined him in amazement that anyone could escape through such a small opening.

"Who are these women, and how did they arrive here? How in the world did this one escape?" Nikolai yelled.

Soon their surprise grew even greater to hear a nearby female voice, "I think I can answer some of your questions." As they peered more closely at a shadowy figure emerging closer to them, the men shared more disbelief. Apparently much more confident than she felt, Marcie presumptively asked, "What? Do you not speak English?" Seeing merely startled faces gave her a small victory and renewed her confidence.

"Who are you?" Capo demanded.

"Who are you people?" With equal force, she asked, "And why treat us like enemies? If you bring my companion from her captivity and begin to treat us with respect, we will talk freely to you. We are no threat to three grown men."

Capo considered this briefly and, with a firm nod toward Ivan, directed him to bring forth their prisoner. Geena had been awed and proud of Marcie's confident attitude as she approached her friend. Marcie promptly asked, "Have they hurt you in any way?"

"No, I'm fine, just a little weak in the knees and tired."

In his interesting mixture of Russian and English, Capo addressed his two comrades. "You searched them when you captured them, I know. This is little threat here. I'll talk to these two in my quarters." Leading them to one of the larger huts, he almost politely invited them, "Please enter."

The area—furnished with a wooden desk, six simple straight-backed chairs, a chest of drawers, and a single bed placed against the back wall— was provisional. Dominating the area was a large assortment of weapons, many carefully arranged on a chest close to the bed. Capo instructed Ivan and Nikolai to remain outside the quarters. Geena offered no indication she understood the conversation as they traded complaints with each other.

Capo assumed the chair behind the desk facing the women, intentionally failing to suggest they sit as well. Marcie, however, endeavored to maintain the momentum of her confidence by sharply asking, "How long have you and your group been on this planet?"

He simply replied without hesitation, "We arrived in February of this year." Geena reflected to herself that would place their arrival barely three months before their own.

Marcie continued as if she were in control, "What is your mission?"

Surprisingly, he complied with her request for further information. "We are on a special assignment by the Russian Space Agency to expand diplomatic endeavors outside the Earth for the benefit of all nations."

Geena struggled to maintain a poker face, confident he was lying.

"As you have no doubt discovered, this planet has qualities surprisingly like those of ours," Capo proclaimed. "We are striving to evaluate the effectiveness of not just survival but colonization or settlement here."

Geena interrupted, "I see you have many weapons. Are you hostile? Are your intentions peaceful?"

"We are not hostile. The weapons you see are for our own protection. We don't know the extent of possible threats. There might be animosity from other living creatures or maybe later on."

Geena struggled to hide her utter disbelief at his comments in an attempt to portray interest.

"Now it is my turn. What are you two ladies doing here?"

"Actually, we are here for scientific research and exploration, much like your initial comments. We are especially concerned with geology and plants, areas of our academic specialties," Marcie replied.

The two women elaborated at least some, adding specialized jargon rarely understood outside their peer groups with similar education and skills. Their motive was a deliberate move to confuse Capo. He at least seemed to accept their comments, merely reflecting acceptance and interest.

"Where is your base?"

"It is about four hundred Earth miles north of where we are now," Geena replied.

"Are there others in your group?" Capo was almost guileless while directing his gaze again toward Geena.

Not wanting to falsify details or facts that might later be discovered and discredit their credibility, the two women acknowledged that another scientist had remained at their lab to analyze and prepare their findings for final reporting. Geena was careful not to express any more detail in her reply than she deemed necessary.

Outside the building, Nikolai and Ivan were debating the trustworthiness of the two women. As the women emerged from their extensive meeting with Capo, Geena heard Nikolai firmly declare, "Those two are deceitful and cannot be trusted!"

Before Ivan had a chance to reply, Capo began his comments to the other two men in Russian, unaware that Geena understood the language. "Gentlemen, what we have here are two qualified American scientists offering their services. Their research will supplement our own. They can be tremendously helpful and are offering their findings to us. We are to help and support them."

Nikolai's disbelief was obvious. "How do we know we can trust them?"

"Because I have decided it," Capo curtly demanded.

Not that far away from the conversation, Marcie and Geena exchanged glances. Both knew by then who has to be won over.

Ivan escorted them to a stone hut in the center of the housing group. There he explained they are welcome to rest and relax but to remain inside until given further instructions. "You are our guests, not our enemies," he concluded.

Once alone, Marcie looked at Geena. "Sure we are guests, at least until we try to leave."

Summarizing what the men had spoken in Russian, Geena brought her friend up to speed. Removing the radio from its concealment, Geena contacted Colonel Engels as Marcie served as lookout through a tiny opening at the entrance of their new home.

"Colonel, the one called Nikolai is intelligent and ruthless. He is our biggest threat. No doubt, he is waiting for us to slip up."

"What does Marcie think?"

"We discussed that. She remembered the old mafia term of *leader* being close to that term *Capo*. He's not wearing gloves and almost seems to have the hands of an artist. No doubt, he sculpted the statue we came across. We both agree he is likely to be American. Ivan is an obedient follower. The three are all intelligent in different ways, but I'm pretty sure the most dangerous one is Nikolai."

"Be careful of that observation, Geena. Remember Ted Bundy. Looks and charm can be misleading. He may be the meek one underneath."

After giving Engels a brief summary of the past few hours, Geena promptly returned her radio to a concealed pocket in her trouser pant leg.

Ivan reappeared to help them explore their surroundings. "We want you to be comfortable here."

It doesn't take long to examine a nearby building with crude but workable plumbing for bathroom and shower needs. A large painted blue water tank sat positioned nearby.

"My goodness," Marcie declared, "you people sure know how to make things nice."

Geena turned away, tongue in cheek.

"This was our first project," Ivan admitted with quiet pride, justifying any slight fault they may have had with the building. "I'm sure you have seen the little people. They are most useful with proper direction."

Not wanting to disclose specific details, Geena merely nodded. "How did you find the little ones?" she asked.

"Several of our cosmonauts had told us about them. We had a few details, however, and no proof until we arrived."

"What controls them? Do they communicate with each other?"

"They are programmed to perform specific assignments. Once that programming wears off, they need reprogramming, or they can communicate with one another and become a potential threat to our plans."

"Do they speak?"

"They make sounds that we cannot understand."

"What about gender? They all seem to be male."

"The females were sent away for a safety measure."

Marcie questioned. "What do you mean 'sent away'? Sent away by whom? And safety—safety from what?"

Ivan responded, "The females are now located a hundred miles or so from here in a development which fits their needs. They have food and plenty of fresh water. We separated the genders at present for better programming of the males while this construction is taking place."

"Let me get this clear"—Geena's voice portrayed open irritation—"I understand that the females among these little people were sent away so that your group could have complete control over the males. No doubt, separating the two genders helps reinforce your authority and power."

Marcie interrupted in an effort to hide some of Geena's outburst, "I believe what Ivan is telling us is that they want to protect both males and females. No doubt, the presence of people from Earth doing things they fail to understand could become upsetting for these people. Ivan, Geena takes exception to treating females unfairly."

"Yes, I was married once and was never treated as an equal." Embarrassed by the feebleness of her explanation, Geena hoped Ivan bought it.

"I understand, ladies," Ivan replied with observable acceptance.

Once back in their assigned quarters, the two women relaxed. The almost barren room provided two cots, a couple of chairs, and a small table. Soon the sound of a challenge confronted their temporary quiet. Without further notice, Nikolai entered and violently tossed two backpacks toward the cots. Surprisingly, he made no comment but abruptly turned on his heel and left them alone.

"At least we have some of our belongings back," Marcie commented.

Furtively contacting Colonel Engels, they asked him to alert Angela.

"I am concerned they may want to verify that another woman scientist is at the base as we indicated," Geena explained.

"Have they mentioned anyone from their group missing?" Colonel Engels asked.

"No, not yet," Marcie replied and concluded with a promise to let him know if they hear that from the men.

After a much-needed rest, they awakened to the sound of marching footsteps. The KEBOWS are marching past the circle of huts, no doubt on the way to the more recent construction site where the women saw the larger scale of weapons.

"I have brought food," Capo called out to the women.

"Great," they both responded in unison and eagerly accepted the rations he had brought.

"Geena, I want you come with me. I have something to show you."

Geena surmised how ominous that might be and glanced at Marcie who spoke up, "We think it better not to separate."

"Relax, Marcie, I promise she will be safe, and I want you to talk to Nikolai, and the two of you get to know each other."

"What! Are you out of your mind?" she blurted. "He doesn't like anyone, not even himself."

"That's almost true, but it shouldn't be a terrible challenge for someone as smart as you."

Marcie carefully pondered on this assignment as Geena obediently followed Capo out of the compound. Aided by their jet-packs, Geena and Capo quickly approached the statue, which had reminded her of *The Thinker*. Capo asked with scarcely concealed pride, "What do you think"

"I think it is a wonderful impressive piece," she replied honestly. "It reminds me of Rodin."

"Yes, you are right. I was early inspired by his work."

"This is an amazing piece of sculpture to find anywhere, especially here in space. How did you manage such fine detail without proper tools?"

"I was an accomplished sculptor at a previous time and always have some of my tools handy."

"What does the inscription mean?" Striving to keep on his good side, she continued to express more interest.

Capo explained that he was in the United States Coast Guard for a number of years when much younger. "I never forgot their motto."

"What about the initials?" she continued to delicately probe. "Are they your initials?"

Nodding, he parried more direct questions. "No, Capo doesn't start with a *K*. It is merely a nickname my comrades have given me."

Geena was aware of his reluctance to give his name or elaborate further. It had become increasingly difficult not to show her anxiety to him.

"I want us to head to your laboratory and for you to introduce me to the other scientist friend you mentioned. You understand we must help and trust one another," Capo demanded.

"It sounds as if you have doubts about our intentions and honesty," Geena guardedly replied.

Capo did not answer but merely abruptly directed her to lead the way. Keeping the existence of her own communication device secret, Geena did not alert Angela of their impending arrival.

Left to her own devices, Marcie immediately began investigating the men's camp. Her former captors were curiously missing. *Now Geena and Capo are going on some secret rendezvous for who knows what, where, or how long! I hope he doesn't plan to seduce her*, she worried.

Marcie quickly contacted Engels and brought him up-to-date. "Colonel, I've found a building here which has all the makings of a workshop. In addition to typical carpentry tools, some seem very unusual." She continued to provide more details of her discovery.

"Thanks, it looks as if they plan to do more extensive construction there, perhaps something more permanent. See what else you can find. How far are you from where the group settled?"

"I don't know, I'll try to learn that as I get the opportunity."

"Did they leave you alone?"

"Yes, but I don't know for how long. I think it best for you to notify Angela to be prepared in case Geena might be forced to bring her escort to the lab.

"Good thinking, Marcie, I'm on it."

"I need to sign off. I hear voices. Someone has been sent to check on me."

➤➤●◄◄

Colonel Engels found Angela in an exceptionally good mood. "What's going on?"

"I m so happy to hear from you; Actually, I'm happy to hear from anyone. Without Marcie and Geena, everything is too quiet here."

"Get prepared," he instructed, bringing her up to date. "You may have company soon. We think that one of the men may insist that Geena take him to your lab."

"That makes a lot of sense. He'll want to learn everything he can about us and what we're up to, no doubt," she acknowledged.

"Angela, just be very careful. If and when they show up, watch what you say. Act surprised to see anyone else human. Remember, no matter how kind he may appear, Geena is in the hands of a criminal. He will no doubt try to exercise control over the three of you. Do all you can to remain together and to stay where you are. Finally, it is imperative for you to keep your radio for us to keep in touch."

"I will. Thanks for the warnings."

With extreme care, Angela again surveyed the lab with renewed concern for anything that might raise suspicion. Anything beyond scientific equipment and recordings would bring obvious repercussions. Convinced that all is in order, she began to notify Mission Control of what had been happening with her counterparts and what they now expected.

"Jon," she explained, "Geena and Marcie are no longer in actual confinement. However, Colonel Engels reminded me that they are under very close observation."

"Angela, it makes a lot of sense that they want to examine your base of operations. Be sure you have only scientific equipment there. This will help confirm that you are focused on geological and biological factors on Europedus. Let me know anything else as soon as you can. Watch yourself!" Jon urged.

———⪼●⪻———

In the meantime, Marcie was having a problem of her own. The irritating man, Nikolai, the one she can't help but think of as the mean one, had begun to harass and interrogate her. No doubt, he intended to intimidate her to become obedient.

She refused to surrender. She boldly looked him in the eye with defiant challenge, "How dare you address me in that tone of voice? You are nothing but a despicable oaf."

Jolted by this brazen attitude, Nikolai suddenly backed away, to the obvious amusement of Ivan.

"What, no comment?" Ivan was almost amused that he hadn't provoked further resentment on the part of his Russian companion. He tried not to keep laughing and risking further anger from Nikolai.

Marcie decided that this would be a good time to try to leave. It might be wise to put some distance between her and the mean one, with his much greater size, strength, and anger. Nikolai merely glanced scornfully at Ivan while pointedly ignoring Marcie heading into one of the stone huts. With ill-concealed gratitude, Marcie walked away in a mixture of relief and loathing toward Nikolai.

Once inside one of the stone huts, Marcie was tired of waiting. The watch on her wrist had apparently finally crawled the two consecutive twelve-hour periods to make up a day. Although, increasingly troubled by concern over Geena's safety, she dared not risk the chance to contact her by radio. Capo would then be aware of the radio's existence and, no doubt, seize it. Instead, Marcie contacted Engels with a clear whisper, "Colonel, can you hear me? I have heard nothing from Geena."

"Marcie, it is not time to panic. You can make it. You are a levelheaded, strong person."

She related her run-in with Nikolai. "He's rash and crude and a giant of a man physically. No doubt, he is about as morally evil as anyone I've encountered. However, here I am standing up to him!"

"Marcie, I care and I am concerned, but let's focus on what we can do. Concentrate on getting more information for us. We are preparing to attack the enemy camp soon. We must gain as much intelligence as we can, particularly about their plans. At the same time, we must thwart the current programming to gain cooperation from the KEBOWS."

"Colonel, I hear Geena. She's louder than usual. They are returning, and she is alerting me."

Engels communication went suddenly silent. Marcie emerged from her hut, expecting to greet Geena and the one they call Capo. To her amazement, Angela was with them.

Capo spoke. "So now we have all of your crew together, right?"

Ivan and Nikolai, who approached when hearing voices, immediately joined them.

Angela strived to keep a poker face as she embraced Marcie. It is Geena who smoothly commented, "Capo thought it safer for everyone if the three of us are together rather than separated. It is easier to protect us all this way. Perhaps even these KEBOWS might be a danger if not influenced by the proper guidance they've been experiencing."

Ivan offered the three women food and beverages, which they gratefully accepted.

After a brief conversation with his comrades, Capo announced, "We have lost one of our own, a comrade who is vital to our mission."

Carefully, controlling their features, the three women realized that they had learned Karl was missing. Instantly grateful that they had not tried to hide him in the lab, Geena casually asked. "Who is missing?"

"His name is Karl Romanov, one of our staff. He's very capable and bright, but I am still concerned. Possibly, he has gotten lost, but some of the native inhabitants may have harmed him if they had not been able to experience our guidance. Also, he may have difficulty with the extremes of temperature without the proper clothing or food for any length of time."

A HAVEN OF ENCHANTMENT

———◦———

After permitted to return to where Marcie and Geena were previously assigned, the women began quietly comparing notes.

"What happened?" Marcie quickly asked.

"Capo first led me to the sculpture we saw. I was careful not to
admit we had seen it before. He was so busy bragging on himself
I doubt if he would have questioned this at all. Then he switched
to direct questions about where our lab is located and how to
locate our associate, meaning you, Angela."

At her glance to Angela, the latter began, "When Capo and I
encountered each other, I probably didn't succeed as well as you
to avert his suspicions. My pretense of astonishment of seeing
another human being wasn't enough to convince him, I fear. He
focused on every inch of our lab before inspecting our communication center and 'accidentally' disabling it. Geena and I both
yelled at him, but he just smiled and claimed that he was doing
us a favor."

Geena continued the account. "Capo commanded Angela to
gather her necessary gear and prepare to leave with us. When she
protested, he loudly informed us that it was not a request. Girls,
I believe we have become prisoners of war, in one that has yet to
be fought."

Upon impulse, Geena decided to glance quickly outside the
entrance. To her surprise, she saw no one at all. The three of
them agreed to take their most necessary belongings and escape,

an impulsive, desperate move. Almost as an afterthought, they decided that if they are caught, they would pretend to investigate the rock, soil, and flora of the area, as disingenuous as that claim might be.

"Colonel, this was almost too easy," Marcie related after the three of them had gained some distance from the huts amidst denser shrubbery. "Why would they leave us without a guard?"

"You hit the nail on the head," he agreed. "This was certainly no accident. They know that you are under their control and that they can recapture you with little effort. I will assume that this Capo person is giving himself more credit than he deserves. Still, be very careful and alert to everything around you. My team and I will be nearby. Our goal now is to get to the rockets and disable them as quickly as possible. You three must pave the way. Go to the tower, determine if it is currently guarded and if necessary, create a diversion so that we can better approach, attack and obtain possession."

"We understand."

Heading toward the tower, the three women, suddenly hampered by a fierce sand storm, quickly lost their bearing in the forceful gusts and flying debris. They had no idea where they were. Just as suddenly, the storm passed, and they saw glimpses of a completely unfamiliar landscape.

Marcie drew their attention to a clump of foliage on the edge of a huge lake. Surveying the area more closely, they excitedly noticed some hilly areas amid the uniformly flat area and some almost familiar stone huts.

"There must be a hundred of these huts," Marcie quickly declared on her radio. "Colonel, you won't believe what we have stumbled across." She explained their experiences in the storm and the result. "For all intents and purposes, we are lost."

"Look around with extreme caution," in a deliberately calm voice, Engels instructed them. "Find out if anyone or anything is there with you."

The three women cautiously approached the stone structures, expecting the unexpected when it happened. Without warning, a small human-like figure emerged from one of the huts. About four feet tall, it was most likely a female of the KEBOWS they encountered before. The figure stopped and intently stared at them. She walked closer to them calmly and obviously unafraid.

Geena quietly relayed everything to Engels. Marcie, stunned and speechless for a moment, gestured for the creature to speak.

The stranger gracefully placed her hand near her chest and said distinctly, "Enid."

Marcie replied by putting her own hand to her chest and repeated clearly, "Marcie."

The three women were amazed and delighted at once. Enid had shown no fear. Next, she motioned for them to follow her to one of the nearby huts. The women looked at one another for mutual approval before following.

Geena was the first to regain her breath. "She smiled when she repeated Marcie's name."

"I noticed she has nice soft features, except I didn't see any eyebrows. Oh, and her ears are virtually flattened against her head."

"Her feet seem larger in proportion to the rest of her," Angela observed.

Reporting more details to Engels, Geena added, "Her clothing appears to be made from animal hides, draping much of her in an almost flattering way. Footwear is almost that of a primitive Native-American style or knee-high moccasin. Her silver hair is short, seems very clean, and glistening. Her teeth are beautifully positioned and very white."

"What about eye contact?"

"She appears comfortable looking directly at us and expecting us to do the same. She seems completely unafraid. So far, we haven't seen any of the other creatures like her."

"Keep me posted," he replied. "We're about ready to stake out the tower."

Rejoining Marcie and Angela, the three followed Enid into one of the huts. Directed to sit on primitive but padded stone benches, they glanced curiously about. The benches appeared to be covered with the same sort of hides they noticed as Enid's clothing. Once seated, Enid offered them a beverage in simple cups poured from a clay container. Unusually trusting, they gratefully began to sip the liquid. It was quite good with a semisweet, fruity taste, cool and refreshing.

The next few hours found effective efforts to achieve increased communication with Enid.

"She is delightfully intelligent," Angela noted with pleasure. Quietly to herself, she added her approval of Enid's attractiveness in a basic and nice way.

"It hasn't taken her any time to learn our names and understand many of our gestures."

Enid then stood with her palms facing them. She clearly wanted them to remain as she quickly exited the hut. Soon, she reentered with several other KEBOWS dressed as she was. Enid indicated each of the three women from Earth and repeated their names in turn so that her fellow KEBOWS understood.

The scientists noted that the women were all extremely polite and appreciative of gracious attention. They had bright, shining eyes, but little noticeable color like brown or blue. Facial skin was smooth, with pale complexions. All had short silky hair, and they appeared almost ageless.

In transmitted text form, Geena informed Engels, "All of the KEBOW women quickly repeated their names and eagerly learned the names of their Earthly visitors. Most are basic four letter names, including *Ishi, Rava, Gara, Ecid*, etc."

"Find out who leads the group and focus on that one for now," he suggested.

"Enid is definitely the one they respect and follow."

At the sound of male voices, Angela quickly warned the others, although the KEBOW women seemed to have heard it even before the women from Earth. Only Enid, with wary eyes, remained near them as the others scattered in panic. Enid slid a narrow, almost hidden panel at the back of the hut and motioned for her three new friends to enter.

"What, you want us to go in there?" Marcie's reluctance was almost palpable as the other women shared concern.

Enid nodded and firmly stated "Go! Go!" much as she had repeated new names. The voices from outside became louder as the women hastily obeyed Enid's command. Instantly, Enid followed, pulling the panel back neatly to conceal the opening.

They found themselves entering an underground passageway with rough, low-ceilinged dimensions and little room to proceed except one at a time. Yet soon a virtual intersection, revealed by Enid's lantern, led in a variety of ways.

"These people are not as primitive as I had thought," Marcie murmured to the other two. They are not able to travel quickly. All know that extreme danger exists if caught.

Finally, Enid climbed a ladder made from twisted branches and hemp-like twine. With Enid's help, they emerged one by one from the tunnels onto a higher peak and into a copse of thick shrubs virtually dwarfed trees near a lake.

"At this point, I don't know if she is astutely aware of dangers for her tribe as well or if she is determined to keep us out of harm's way." Catching her breath, Marcie radioed Colonel Engels with a briefing. Enid listened intently.

"Marcie, I want the three of you to concentrate on learning how to communicate more with Enid. Try any combination of words, gestures, body language, things like that, which might help."

"Colonel, we know that she wants to communicate as desperately as we do. We have already made a great deal of progress as she hangs on every word."

"Good! I'll get back to you. We are nearing the tower and will try to keep you informed too."

After listening to Marcie's conversation, Enid pulled a raft-type boat moored near them and hidden within thickets of dense shrubbery. The women from Earth were fascinated at how quickly and efficiently all this had been done.

"What do you suppose she wants us to do?" Geena asked when they saw the small craft and what appeared, as oars.

Enid grasped the meaning of Geena's question and waved for them to follow. Pointing to the raft, she verbalized to each in turn with a single word, *boat*.

"Enid, do you want us to get in the boat?" Marcie simply asked.

Enid pointed again. "Get in boat, Marcie. Get in boat, Angela. Get in boat, Geena. Get in boat."

Geena smiled broadly in appreciative surprise as she led the others onto the craft. Enid firmly pushed the boat away from the shore before hopping aboard. Handing an oar to each of the others, she began to row with determination and care rather than speed. The women noted that, no doubt, Enid an old hand at this method of travel.

"Where is she taking us?" Marcie asked as if she would get an answer. Angela and Geena looked at one another and almost laughed at the absurdity of what they were doing as Marcie continued, "I can't believe we are sailing on a lake to who knows where with someone that isn't quite like us and that this is taking place in such a place. There have been constant threats of destruction and danger here, what is going to happen next?"

Enid joined the laughter as if she knew exactly what they were saying. Further conversation helped strengthen the bonds, trust, and increased understanding as Enid and the other women spoke with each other.

An unusual breeze created something almost like a current on the lake, nudging them along with some guidance and further propulsion by their rowing. Much of the lakeshore revealed an extensive variety of vegetation of all sorts, sizes, and colors. Angela and her two counterparts noted how unusual the variety of greenery competed for their attention with their general curiosity of their revealed destination.

Enid skillfully guided their small craft through almost transparent waters. Soon the three Earth women, delighted by the view of color change, experienced an almost emerald brilliance in the atmosphere.

"It is as if the path is leading to a garden of delight," Angela declared.

"This is a far cry from my little prison accommodation," Marcie reminded them.

Enid's reassuring looks displayed a prideful smile as the women increasingly delighted by what they were seeing.

"There is virtually no way to say how amazing this is," Geena whispered. "Remember what we learned from the book of Psalms, 'The Heavens declare the glory of God.'"

"Geena, I believe you have aptly spoken for all of us," Marcie admitted.

Time seemed to both crawl and fly by for them. Suddenly Enid indicated a specific position along the shoreline ahead of them. With quiet efficiency, she pounced off the boat, securing it safely to a wooden mooring. The dock led to a small area with thick vegetation competing for any place to disembark for them. Enid motioned them through a dense, shoulder-height field of weeds before they reached a clearing. From there, appeared landscapes and geological formations different from any they had encountered so far.

The clearing was a flat grassy area with a deeper green hue and about the size of two football fields. There were high hills, almost mountains, surrounding the area on three sides. Opening gaps identified a variety of directions toward the hills. After allowing each to catch their breath, Enid led them purposefully toward one passageway in particular.

Geena spoke to and for the others, "Where in the world—or out of it, I should say—are we going?"

Before entering the passageway, Enid motioned for the others to stay put.

Angela became alarmed. "Do you think there are animals in this area?"

"Angela, based on what we have already seen and experienced, I wouldn't be surprised if we rode out of here on a dinosaur, possibly a flying one."

Geena bent down to examine the soil, learning that it is much less rocky and possibly capable of cultivation compared to what they had experienced. "I'm confident this soil is rich enough for cultivation. In fact, the KEBOWS are obviously farming here. The field we just left had husks similar to our corn."

"Yes," Marcie replied, "I have some of those husks and some of the stalks in my backpack for further analysis if and when we get a chance."

"Wait," Geena interrupted, "Colonel Engels is trying to reach us."

"Where are you, and what is going on?" he questioned.

Geena began a detailed report of their whereabouts and recent experiences. She concluded with her logical observations, "I don't know all the specifics of what to expect from our new friend, but our instincts say to trust her. She knows how severely we were in danger and is working extensively to lead us to safety. What have you learned about Capo and his crew?"

"We have discovered a cache of weapons in a cave near their headquarters," Engels responded. "He is obviously threatened by the three of you. This, aggravated by the loss of one of his men, would be a problem. Either would be a problem, but together could cause him a lot of anxiety. They are desperate to find the three of you. It would be best to stay as far away as possible from where he would expect you to be. Learn as much as you can and let me know. You'll help all of us by gaining any information. In the meantime, we'll continue keeping a close eye on Capo and his group."

After exploring several paths, Enid returned and motioned to the three women. Scarcely breathing, they followed her to a new area. Sparklingly clear air and warm comfortable temperatures delighted all four of them. Light from what appeared as a million stars provided a wonderful spectacle.

"This is beyond remarkable," Geena professed.

Her eyes scanning the sky and horizons, Marcie alleged, "This is what I have always dreamed heaven to be."

Angela followed Enid closely as she beckoned all to follow. "Oh my!" she gasped. "Look at this."

They stopped and stared in amazement at what appeared as a large settlement, almost buried behind walls of overgrown plants.

"I am speechless," Marcie declared. "This is like a space Atlantis, more beautiful than we could imagine."

The stone buildings were significantly larger than any others they had seen on Europedus, with flat roofs and significant architectural embellishments. Most appeared the same color, as if whitewashed by natural weather and elements.

Enid motioned them on as she addressed them by name, "Marcie, Geena, Angela."

"You want us to follow, right?" Geena almost didn't expect an answer but asked anyway as if to provide time for them to consider whether or not to do so.

"Follow." Enid nodded quickly.

The four reached the entrance to one of the five nearest buildings, where Enid pulled away what might be animal skin curtains, giving the others space to enter.

Marcie tried to make Enid understand their concerns. "Is this place safe from Capo?"

Enid, visibly shaken by hearing the name *Capo*, began to shake her head side to side. Pausing to breathe more deeply, she placed her palm near her chest and repeated the word *safe* several times to let them know she understood. She was obviously threatened by the idea of Capo, almost cringing at the thought and negatively repeating the name a few times.

"We get the picture," Geena told her. "Capo or some of his group were getting too close. Enid helped us by taking us to safety."

All three of the women scientists appreciated Enid's intelligence, caring, and assistance. Enid further revealed her growing understanding by repeating, "No Capo here! Safe here!"

Resting and relaxing for a time, the four continued expanding how to understand each other. Words and even sentences soon replaced gestures as they learned more and more. Enid was especially sad that her partner was not with her. She reported that all of the KEBOW men were led away by Capo and other "bad humans," the new phrase Angela taught her.

They reported to Colonel Engels all that they were learning. "There are no other signs of life than we have encountered," Geena reported for the group.

He was delighted by the progress his "three angels," as he had grown fond of thinking of them, had achieved in communicating with Enid. "It sounds as if these KEBOW women were wisely staying in their area so as not to endanger their home village."

Only too soon, Enid indicated she needed to leave them, and head to another part of the village. She gave each a quick hug. "I come back." She promised to return with additional food and other supplies.

"Have the two of you seen little people or children around this village?"

"Angela, these are all little people," Geena answered. "No, I didn't. Perhaps these male and female KEBOWS have been separated for quite some time. I'm starting to think that either Capo is lying about coming to this planet only shortly before us or that he and his men have replaced others. Some of the males may have matured within captivity."

Realizing how hungry they had become while their attention was on communicating with Enid, they settled in to rest in their new quarters and began to munch on what Enid had shown them before. They appeared to be raw vegetables, much like potatoes or similar products.

"These don't taste bad, just different," Angela commented.

"I don't l know what this food is, but it seems to be the only game in town now that our rations are gone."

"Well now, I wouldn't say that," Geena declared as she proudly displayed two bars of chocolate. "We have a heavenly dessert with these!"

It had been a lengthy and tiring day as they settled in to rest. After extensive sharing of immediate observations, the conversation turned to, "I wonder when Enid will reappear."

"Is she for real, or is this all a dream?"

"I vaguely remember coming here, but what year was it?"

All realized how silly they were getting into their comments. They finally eased and drifted into a much-needed sleep.

Henri Boudet, the scout sent by Engels to scout out the other humans, was a tremendous asset to all. His intelligence, knowledge of several languages, and ability to think shrewdly and stay hidden had allowed him to gain a great deal of intelligence about Capo's group.

"Colonel," he began to relate to Engels, "Capo is definitely their leader. He speaks of a ground zero somewhere in central Russia, which is the focus of their control. It is obviously the source of these many threats and support. This Russian headquarters has ordered a variety of activities, including destruction both here on Europedus and on Earth, the disruption of many forms of world currency there, and selective assassinations. They all seem to think this is funny, especially Nikolai."

"Anything else?"

"Yes! Capo has instructed Nikolai to locate the three so-called women scientists and exterminate them as soon as possible."

"Okay. We can't hesitate anymore. Let's locate, capture, and disarm them all and all their equipment."

"Henri, what do you think? What do you think of the KEBOWS?"

"I don't believe it would be helpful to capture them. They have little skill in actually starting and stopping the equipment or altering any of the weapons. They are to maintain everything, keeping it clean and ready for operation. I also think it would be helpful to learn where any of the supporting funding from the United States might originate. Follow the paper trail, so to speak."

"Yes, you're right. Why don't you return to our prisoner, Karl? He has had ample time to think. Besides, he's probably tired of the basic rations we've given him. Take something a little more special, find out what he knows, and suggest a degree of leniency. Tell him we can help. We'll speak up on his behalf once on Earth if he cooperates. Lead him to believe we have the upper hand on Capo and his crew since we do!"

As soon as Henri departed, Colonel Engels began to share his next plans.

"Ladies, we are going to sabotage the machinery and weaponry in the tower with powerful explosive devices. Don't forget, the three of you are on Capo's hit list."

"Thank you, Colonel. We suspected as much", Geena replied. "We will make it and wish all of you Godspeed."

Engels departed with half of his team, heading directly toward the tower. The remaining five men approached as a second wave, directed to follow with various assignments to assist, wrap up, or rescue as appropriate.

—————⟫◉⟪—————

The women scientists had only a short time to fret when comfort arrived from the return of Enid. A friend accompanying Enid, who, upon direction from Enid, put her hand to her chest and stated the name Jeda. After further introductions, all sat and enjoyed the provisions Enid and Jeda had brought.

Geena began to discuss their concern about the tower, gesturing with her arms and hands to help assure the alien women's comprehension. "Enid, Jeda, did Nikolai come anywhere near here?"

The very sound of the name provoked both alien women to anxiously look about and almost shiver. This response was actually more intense than when Enid responded to *Capo* before, clearly revealing their fears.

"No, not come here," Enid finally responded. She went on to explain as well as she could to make them understand that Capo, Nikolai and the others are unaware of this retreat. "You stay here. You safe here," Enid concluded as if it were she who determined what is best for them.

Smiling and feeling more confident after this, Enid and Jeda offered hugs and farewells before slipping away.

CONFRONTING THE ENEMY

———

When Engels and his men reached the tower, one lone sentry revealed anything amiss. From the description by the women, they concluded this sentry must be Nikolai, the fierce one.

"No doubt he's here to exterminate anyone and everyone they feel a threat to their operation, especially the women," Colonel Engels observed. "The women pointed out that although it is Capo, rather than Nikolai, who is actually in charge, he is a serious danger. Capo may make the decisions, but Nikolai delights in carrying them out in the most destructive and torturous methods possible."

Readying for their next steps, all of Engels's crew observed that Nikolai was heavily armed. No evidence existed if anyone was inside the tower. They proceeded directly, intending to divert the villain's attention, as a carefully placed explosive device changed everything. A hidden booby-trap bomb killed one of Engel's men instantly, while another was injured.

The five in a backup group joined them as all aim to where Nikolai had been standing. Unfortunately, Nikolai escaped through a cloud of smoke into the tower. The colonel and his men realized that if anyone else is inside the tower, they had heard the warning and prepared to retaliate.

Meanwhile, while this was going on, Henri reached the compound where the prisoner, Karl, was confined in makeshift jail, hungry and thirsty. He offered the prisoner additional food and water and waited a surprisingly long time before asking him direct questions.

Jon Mattingly became increasingly anxious at Mission Control. With no word from anyone for quite a long time, he feared time is running out. Yet he appreciated the good news he later shared, that a spacecraft had left Cape Canaveral with reinforcements, the arrival details were not yet confirmed.

Engels shared news of their losses to Henri. It was an obvious painful blow. "Henri, go to the lab of our three women and try to repair the damage Capo has done to their communication center and other equipment. If you can, contact Jon Mattingly at NASA. Give him an update, and tell him where the women are and that they are safe for now. Have you learned any more details from Karl?"

"Yes. Capo is definitely in charge. He answers only to Viktor Stanislaus, a former Russian diplomat in Moscow, who has an extremely interesting story. He acquired huge wealth initially as a slumlord and later seems to have his hands in all sorts of cash-rich activities. He is a man of powerful influence. Because of his great power and wealth, he has begun to believe he is above the law in either his country or any other. In effect, his next goal is economic destruction of the United States."

"Please relay everything you have found to NASA. Get Interpol up to speed and involved. They can help locate him despite all his wealth and power."

Relaying this information back to Marcie, Engels voice was brief and direct. "We have casualties. There was an unexpected bomb. One is dead, and one is injured. We currently surround the entire tower but don't know who or what else might be inside in addition to Nikolai, who escaped our first efforts to capture him. Henri headed to your lab to contact NASA. Stay where you are until further notice."

"I think Enid is confident she can help the male KEBOWS revive from their programming," Marcie exclaimed.

Enid's response confirmed this. "Come follow," she briskly instructed them. They immediately did so. All three women from Earth knew that she had become a helpful comrade and friend. Quickly, they all boarded an available boat and soon rejoined the other KEBOW women on a shoreline clearing some distance away.

"Enid is explaining that we will be leaving them, and they should say farewell," Marcie shared her belief with Geena and Angela.

"That is so sweet," Geena noted.

"Uh-uh! You are both wrong. They are preparing to come with us," Angela warned. All three women glanced at one another and the KEBOWS for confirmation. "Look, they are gathering up basic gear and heading closer to us."

"Now what? Just how many of them are there?" Marcie questioned.

"I count at least thirty-six," Geena answered. "We can't let this happen. It's not right to risk their lives and safety."

Their efforts to convince Enid that the KEBOW women must remain behind fell on virtually deaf ears. Enid listened with polite attention but soon indicated her disagreement by her body language and two-word remarks. "We go! We help!" She was steadfastly determined as were all of the KEBOW women. Soon all of the natives of Europedus chanted firmly in unison, "We go!"

"Enid, this is very dangerous. You cannot risk yourself and your friends," Geena pleaded.

With even more determination, Enid and all of the others continued, "We go!"

The three American women realized they had to decide not to go at all or take everyone.

"If Engels and the others are in jeopardy, we must help. Let's hope the old idea of safety in numbers applies here," Geena stated.

Marcie threatened to panic. "If anything happens to the colonel and his group, how will any of us survive?"

With no more time to lose, all followed Enid, who steadfastly headed toward the tower. Behind Enid and the three women from Earth, the band of KEBOWS followed in tow two by two.

———————

Colonel Dawson Engels continued directing quite a bit of activity. The wounded soldier had been located nearby at a small oasis and out of harm's way. Most of the other crew were following the colonel, advancing toward the tower, ever watchful for a bomb or mine. He instructed the five men in the backup crew to follow them after a brief amount of time and space, with the exception of the last man who was to remain as lookout.

The explosion had left a lot of dusty residue. Otherwise, the air remained clean under a magnificent starlit sky. The colonel's crew again focused on the task at hand, eliminating the danger of Nikolai and any others who might have been with him inside the tower.

Engels reminded himself, *This is not just any criminal. This person is pure evil, determined to bring death, destruction, and chaos to the earth. There is no honorable martyrdom here.*

The colonel, the first to reach the tower entrance, motioned to his crew where they were to locate. Suddenly with great strength, he charged against the metal protective shield in front of the tower. The shield crashed to the ground. Swiftly, he lunged away from the opening, right before a burst of retaliatory machine-gun fire from inside would have obliterated anyone still in front of the door.

Crawling through the entrance under the temporary camouflage of gun smoke, Engels's keen eyes saw a moving dark object partially obscured by weapons. He fired, and there was a deep groan, followed by a crash and then complete silence. Nikolai was no longer a threat.

Turning to his crew, Engels reminded them, "We're not out of the woods yet. We still have those we regard as Ivan the Terrible and Capo the Clown to deal with. And that is not to mention all those little people and any programmed threat they may offer. It is imperative that we succeed. As quickly as possible, disarm all of this weaponry and potential war equipment. Dismantle everything, and destroy major parts. However, be very careful. Don't trigger anything like that previous explosion."

The sentry who had remained behind and outside of new danger soon alerted them, "There are loud sounds of troops approaching, quite probably an advance of reinforcements for Nikolai."

Engels calmly ordered, "Keep disabling this equipment, no matter what happens." Turned directly to the sentry, he asked, "How many are there?"

"I'm not sure, but there is clearly a sound of a lot of movements, like a small army."

"Okay, men, take up your arms and prepare to defend yourselves and all of us from attack if they get closer. We don't know what weapons they have, so be vigilant. They are coming to defend or, as it turns out now, take back the tower. Be prepared to stay here unless I give specific directions otherwise. We'll find out soon enough just what they are planning I'm sure."

The sentry returned to inform them of numerous shadowy figures approaching. Engels tried to radio the women, who he thinks are still safe at the KEBOW women's retreat. "There seems to be interference in all radio channels," he decided. The rest of his crew agreed. "We'll try again soon, but right now, we have other problems."

"Colonel Engels!" The lookout sentry's voice almost cracked like an adolescent teen's in his surprise and excitement. "The KEBOW men are all surrounding the tower. They have uniform white jumpsuits on, and each has a metallic shield. There are so many of them, almost impossible to count."

"Is anyone else with them, someone from Earth?"

"Not that I can see, only the KEBOWS."

Without warning, one of the little people wandered closer to the tower. The sentry grabbed him with surprising speed and brought him to an abrupt halt. Firmly grasping the little alien by his forearm, he thrust him into the tower.

Engels carefully scrutinized the newcomer. As before, he noticed how similar to humans the KEBOW appeared, but on a smaller, less-detailed scale. The colonel inspected the shield that he had been holding. The KEBOW's only response was a repetitious motion of his arms near his face. A small handheld device dropped from his hand.

"It's some variation of a stun gun. He is not likely to be much of a threat without it. He seems still to be a bit out of it anyway." Engels picked up the KEBOW as if he were a child about to be reprimanded and placed him in a dark corner nearby. He was submissive, remaining quiet, almost dazed. For some moments, the entire area remained similarly quiet, both inside and outside the tower.

———————

The women traveled with amazing speed, covering significant water and land distances in their determination to help at the tower. All were confident, both of the need to help and of their abilities to do so.

"I am still concerned. We can't reach them with this radio," Marcie remarked, not for the first time.

Concerned but confident, the other women from Earth, Enid, and all the KEBOW women continued tirelessly and with obvious courage as they approached closer.

Without warning, Marcie and Geena lost balance and tumbled into a depression, which they had been unable to see. Two of the KEBOW women tried to stop them from falling and ended up falling after them into the darkness.

Angela, Enid, and the others quickly struggled desperately to find any way to help their fallen comrades and bring them to safety. Yet at least initially, it didn't seem as if there was any way to do so.

———>●<———

Henri had been working steadily and proficiently, repairing the satellite communication systems at the lab. By a stroke of luck and by his expertise, he finally succeeded. His initial contact was to Jon Mattingly, who delighted to hear from anyone in the crew.

"Henri, what is happening? I have had no contact with anyone forever. Do you know any details?" Jon asked anxiously.

"At the assault on the enemy's stronghold at the tower, two of our men were injured, one fatally. Everyone else is safe for now and currently inside the tower. The one-enemy combatant called Nikolai is deceased," Henri reported.

"What about the women?"

"The last I heard, they were somewhere else. Unfortunately, they have not been in radio contact. They were with the KEBOW women at an isolated retreat. Engels told them to stay put because of extreme danger."

"Henri, you must stay where you are to keep all our lines of communication as open as possible. Colonel Engels is capable and resourceful."

"I agree. Just recently, during intermittent radio contact, he indicated that Ivan and Capo are not alone or won't be for long. Others are on their way to Europedus, just as we have reinforcements coming here."

"What about the KEBOW men?" Jon inquired.

"That is a very perplexing point," Henri admitted. "When the enemy has them controlled, there is a greater danger. They are numerous, and they have protective shields and basic stun guns. Engels thinks he has a better handle on them. One KEBOW is in captivity. He is offering no resistance and showing signs of awakening from a hypnotic state or deep sleep."

"Okay! Keep in contact with all of them and with me as often as possible. Be sure to regain contact with our three women. Stay in touch."

"Over and out."

Partially relieved by his conversation with Mattingly, Henri, nevertheless, was reminded of shared anxiety. Both were obviously concerned about what was happening with the women.

———————

When Colonel Dawson Engels and his additional backup crew entered the tower, all saw the small KEBOW huddled in the corner. The dwarf-like figure had almost transparent hair, extremely smooth complexion, and ears very close to his head. Probably due to the increased attention directed his way, the creature seemed to pay a greater amount of attention to the men from Earth.

"I am Dawson, what is your name?" Engels repeated the process with patient persistence until the KEBOW began to imitate him. Just as Engels placed his hand in front of his chest, there is a similar response.

"Adow, I am Adow," the creature replied.

Engels rewarded his new acquaintance with a huge grin and further encouragement. It is as if Adow's alertness had grown with the relative darkness and opportunity to interrelate with others, even if the others are from Earth.

He is quick actually, Engels thinks to himself. *Whatever has dulled their apparent senses and virtually programmed them is penetrable. It' as if extreme sources of certain light outs them into other's control, what we've been calling programmed trances. Repeated encounters with the same sort of light continue the effect.* Almost as an aside, he noticed the beautiful expanse of white teeth the KEBOW revealed in returning his smiles, something that would give credit to any dentist.

The colonel and his men began leading several of the KEBOW men into the tower. Soon many of them huddled next to Adow. It didn't take long to confirm Engel's beliefs soon, as more and more of the KEBOWS became increasingly alert and less automatic.

"Just as I suspected, this darkened space has interrupted their programming. Let's keep them together and help bring them to realize they can trust us. They do seem to respect Adow, probably as their leader," Engels informed his men.

With little to go on except the reports from their women scientists, Engels suddenly remembered the name of one of the alien women. At first mention of the name *Enid*, Adow's face became animated and more alert. With patient concern, Engels was able to communicate that Enid and the other KEBOW women were safe.

"Now we have to assure them we are here to help, which we are. No doubt, they aren't fond of the terrorists," Engels added.

The KEBOWS increasingly paid more attention to their counterparts from Earth and what they were saying. Yet in an ironic side effect, they continually repeated their own and other's names in their eagerness to communicate with these new strangers from Earth.

Encouraged by their quickness and energy, Engels related to his crew, "Let's help get them focused. They must understand that we need their help. Without their help, they are in at least as much danger as the rest of us."

Gesturing solely toward Adow, Engels and he engaged the KEBOWS focus and loyalty. The KEBOW men previously distanced from their women and programmed to become hostile toward others under the terrorists' control, comprehended more clearly. How crucial it was for everyone's survival that they all cooperate with these new Earth creatures. Soon they were assisting in the dismantling of the remaining weaponry in the tower. Attention soon directed upon what happened next.

They didn't have long to wait—Capo, Ivan and a group of several troops were approaching from a rendezvous several miles away. They came to a sudden halt when within sight of the tower. Capo became alarmed.

There was complete silence. Where are the KEBOWS, and why don't they hear the usual sound of marching feet? Especially of concern was the absence of the women they had earlier imprisoned, and others thought of as eventual threats.

Partial alleviation of that concern was if the women are no longer in the picture. "After all, what can three helpless women do to mess up our plans? Nikolai has probably taken care of them, possibly blowing himself up in the process," Capo remarked. Capo was actually more concerned about the location of the KEBOWS. "We must locate them before their programming ends!"

His irritation had only grown as they approached the tower to see no sign of anything at all. He called out, "Nikolai?"

There was no response.

As the group marched closer, they noticed missing shields and portions of covers left to obscure the entrance. Halting several paces away, Capo commanded Ivan to check on Nikolai. Ivan's cautious initial inspection inside revealed a group of KEBOWS all grouped in silence looking directly into his eyes, all with completely different expressions than ever before.

Boldly, the KEBOWS spaced their metallic shields in shared protection. With confused frustration, Ivan determined to enter and not risk Capo's wrath. He entered the tower, only to become swiftly captured. As if bagging a bird in flight, Engels men gagged and restrained Ivan so quickly there was no time to call out or warn anyone outside what had happened. Ivan was efficiently escorted to a darkened back area of the tower where the colonel and his men began purposeful interrogation.

Engels was of two minds at this point. As productive as it might be to lead the others to enter for ambush, he realized Ivan might have a way to warn them. Reluctantly deciding to patiently wait, the colonel and his team were at least partially relieved that Ivan had only one older-model rifle.

Believing the KEBOWS might have become a threat and ultimately detained Ivan, Capo instructed a group of five from his crew to intimidate the aliens. "Find what they are up to and what is going on with Nikolai. Their weapons will be meager compared to your strength and arms."

Keeping steadily on the alert, Engel's crew, along with the KEBOWS, quickly captured the five villains.

"This is almost too easy," one of the younger team members remarked. "It's like plucking apples off a tree."

Suddenly a shot rang out, creating confusion and warning everyone outside of danger. Before helping the colonel and the others, some of his team secured their prisoners into large containers previously used to hold weapons. The KEBOWS, with Adow's help and the colonel's direction, exited the tower, marching two by two as they consistently did.

Capo could not believe his eyes. The shielded KEBOWS were encircling Capo's men, boldly knocking away many of their weapons, and nudging them directly into the tower. Striving to ignore the aliens, Capo and his remaining men directed their weapons toward the tower. Desperately trying to maintain control, they faced the perils of surprise, inadequate support, and loss of manpower. Yet they were determined to advance, trying to convince themselves that they would succeed.

REUNITED

As the women reached the tower, Engels and his crew and the male KEBOWS were exiting. The women from Earth wondered just how long the KEBOW men and women had been separated from one another. Yet the obvious delight of both groups in seeing each other again was well appreciated by all. Engels was visibly pleased to see that his three angels had survived.

"Bring me up to date," he instructed, directing his request to all, but clearly focusing on Angela.

It is she who related their last few perils, including almost losing the four in the crevice. Her shared appreciation for him and his crew was obvious, as she repeated, "We're so happy to see you again!"

"Ladies, we have been fortunate but still have severe challenges ahead. Our next step is to communicate with NASA."

"What should we do?" Marcie's voice sounded a bit stronger but still moderately weak from her recent ordeal.

"Keep a watchful eye, and go back to your lab. Henri should be there now or should be by the time you get there. We'll take care of these prisoners and secure the tower before any possible reinforcements arrive to help them."

Marcie glanced away and cleared her throat almost silently. She resisted the impulse to ask just what he meant by "taking care of the prisoners." Reluctantly, the women realized that where they are and what has happened has made significant challenges to the Geneva Convention rules. Necessity may require measures they didn't expect.

"Marcie, you and Angela stay together and return to your lab until we return. Geena, I need you here as a translator."

"Yes, Colonel," they agreed.

Meanwhile, the male and female KEBOWS huddled together, giving those from Earth some space. Yet there seemed to be a quick appreciation of their mixed loyalties. Helping the men and women from Earth was still a strong concern, despite the alternative to return to as much of what they were used to as they could. They realized that until the dangers of terrorists are taken care of, they likely will not be truly secure.

Engels appreciated this as he noted their innate intelligence. The more they were involved with humans, the quicker they learned and were able to interact.

Adow's face illuminated as Engels approached him.

"Are their more bad people? Are there other places with machines?" Engels asked, indicating the tower and its contents. "Are there more Capos?"

With a serious expression and almost secret pride in understanding, Adow moved his head from side to side and gestured in the negative. "No, no more. No Capo. No machines."

Engels looked at his men and expressed a further concern. "Since they have been programmed almost like being in a trance, they might not fully understand what I am asking or how to answer."

Enid confidently interrupted, "No more Capo. No more tower.

Enid's clear declaration helped reassure Engels and his men, although some concern lingered. Geena followed her protectors into the tower. Final efforts to subdue Capo and his crew had rendered them captive, if not cooperative. Capo's glimpse of Geena created a growl of disgust. He switched to muttering and talking with his crew in Russian while Geena listened raptly. She learned nothing other than his dismissive blame on those "loath-some women" who betrayed them.

When she had the opportunity, Geena discreetly alerted Engels about other significant details Capo revealed. "A spaceship with armed reinforcements is supposed to arrive within the next two days. He hinted at a controlling big boss, a wealthy backer, but didn't mention his name. Capo alerted his entire group to be constantly prepared for an opportunity of escape."

"Keep listening," he whispered to Geena. "They are so arrogant you may well learn a lot more. As long as we gain useful information, they are important. Once that is over, their days are numbered."

Geena quietly shuddered but realized how true that had become.

Engels's attention turned to the KEBOWS in grateful appreciation that they intended to stay and support his group. Shared discussion with them not only helped the confidence of the men and Geena, but also particularly notable was Enid's offer to bring food.

When Angela and Marcie returned to their lab, they found Henri, who had been anxious to hear from anyone. He looked to them with obvious relief as the two of them related all that had taken place. He told them he had successfully repaired the communication system and contacted Mission Control.

"Mattingly is waiting for updates," Henri stated.

Marcie's report to Jon Mattingly was very comprehensive. They both shared pertinent information from both directions as Angela and Henri listened.

Mattingly's next topic was almost anticipated by more tension in his voice.

"Ladies, as I have told Henri, we are in a race against time. The Secret Service has averted a serious threat to the president of the United States or someone in his family. Interpol and similar agencies are aware of this—which is actually in addition to what you already know about threats there on Europedus.

"We wanted you to be in the loop about all of this since you obviously need and deserve to know. Return to Engels with these specifics. Anything he or Geena can learn from those prisoners is crucial. These people are evil and are determined to bring destruction.

"Our own spaceship is on its way with several troops to help you and the cleanup. This craft should arrive within forty-eight hours. Then within a week or two, the *Freedom Promise* should arrive with the same crew who brought you to Europedus as they have promised to do so. Hang in there! Your mission is nearing successful completion."

"What about the KEBOWS?" Angela asked.

"There has been a lot of discussion on this. What is your take on them, ladies?" You have spent quite a bit of time with them."

"Yes, we have learned to appreciate and respect them for who they are. Once out of their programmed trances, they are alert, caring, and remarkably intelligent. They are a happy tribe and extremely loyal to one another," Angela reported.

"We haven't had enough time to focus on their methods of agriculture or things of that nature since we had other things going on, but they should be fine. They are delighted to have the men and women back together and return to the comfort and security of what they're used to. It is probably best to leave them where they are." Marcie suggested.

"Okay. I will be in touch after your contact with Engels and the others. Please give my regards to Geena too."

Both Angela and Marcie grinned to each other and wink at Henri as they assure Jon Mattingly that they will honor his request.

In reply to Engels's obvious concern, the new arrivals related their communication to Jon Mattingly and Mission Control.

With a grin, Marcie concluded, "Geena, he specifically sent you a special greeting."

Geena attempted, without success to keep a poker face, but her fellow women scientists shared her pleasure.

"What about the prisoners?" Henri's question quickly shifted the focus and the mood.

"We have secured Capo and those with him," Colonel Engels answered. "So far, that seems to be everyone besides Karl, whom we already know about. Geena has been paying close attention to all of their conversations. She has learned a great deal we've needed to know.

"The big boss, Capo, has connections to Viktor Stanislaus, who is evidently the brains and has the money behind all this He's been portrayed in the media as 'the Devil.' He's made little secret of his ruthlessness to gain power and money. He's been able to escape criminal charges, although virtually everyone suspects he's behind much of the Russian black market and assassinations of business and political opponents. Capo indicated that Stanislaus has a huge hidden hideout—known to only a few despite his reputation, even beyond Russia—called the Moons."

"We must get this information to NASA and the other authorities. No doubt, their plot to control this planet is related. Capo and his men speak of rescue from reinforcements who are on their way here. We must intercept their spacecraft before that takes place," Engels urged.

Geena spoke for all of them as she asked, "How can this take place?"

"I don't know for sure, but I feel Mattingly and his crew need to know all of this and can certainly help. Geena, continue to stay close and listen for anything further of any significance. If you can, determine anything specific 'bout that spacecraft."

"I will, Colonel," she concurred.

Engels headed up a group back to the women's lab. In addition to three of his men, Henri and Angela were with them. He directed two of the crewmembers to check on the prisoner, Karl. To their pleasant surprise, he was much more informative, providing specific names and details related to their assignments and the hideout of Stanislaus and his organization. In reply to pointed questions, he revealed that the Moons area was in a large mountain area in the Caucasus Mountains, with guards on duty day and night. The guards equipped with mounted and hand-held weaponry.

Karl revealed that as many as twenty guards were on duty at any given time and that the area specifically used for missile and spacecraft launches. He confirmed that the specific mountain was translated into English as Moon Mountain, hence the name of the hideout. After gathering as much additional information detail as possible, the interrogators provided Karl a greater amount of food and beverage than usual.

Colonel Engels gave an account of all the new details to Jon Mattingly at Mission Control who instantly communicated every detail to the United States sites connected to Secret Service for the White House, Homeland Security, and the FBI. With surprising cooperation, they teamed with security teams assigned by the Russian government to address the threat. Instantly, they cracked guerilla and counter-terror forces headed to the Caucasus Mountain range and focused on Moon Mountain.

Media executives were beside themselves, urgently trying to gain details to feed the twenty-four-hour requirement needed to inform the public. As efficiently as forces mobilized to attack Stanislaus's headquarters, the secrecy was maintained.

Initial surveillance by warplanes revealed little specific detail surrounding Moon Mountain. At a lower altitude, further inspection detected a synthetic covering, allowing the top edge of a large craggy area to slide away from the top of the mountain. It was feasible that a spacecraft could launch in that remote, mountainous area. Distance and unimaginable high-tech instruments had permitted them to escape detection for who knows how long.

Both the United States and Russia assigned tactical special troops to quietly rendezvous and prepare for combat. Cooperation was again shown as few egos or disagreements appeared. All focused on eliminating the clouds of threat over the two nations and humanity.

CONQUERING A MOUNTAIN

Geena could not wait to tell Capo of Karl's informative and willing efforts to save his own skin. Initially, he scowled in disbelief and spat out, "Not true. This is a trick."

"Oh, but it is true." She then began a litany of what they had learned about Moon Mountain. "By the way, the Devil has been killed." Geena used this deception to prompt Capo into divulging further information.

Capo showed little response, merely sneering.

"Capo, you will see," Geena declared while jumping back from the man's efforts to spit on her.

Leaving him to reflect on what she had told him, Geena repositioned herself out of sight, but within hearing range. Capo and his comrades spoke in rapid Russian. It was obvious that their determination to continue their plots against the occupants of Europedus and Earth hadn't lessened. They spoke of loyalty to a higher good and ultimate martyrdom.

"Too bad for them," Geena muttered to herself. Bored by such repeated declaration and intellectual numbness, she almost dozed off until jarred by a further development. Capo's elaboration about reinforcements that were likely to arrive immediately brought her instantly awake. As she headed to find Engels, Geena heard someone call her name.

Enid's left foot appeared caught in a crevice between some rocks, and she was struggling to get free.

"Enid, are you okay?"

"Okay. But…" Enid responded. "Colonel, send me to you, bring water." Then her voice dropped as if in obvious apology. "I drop water. I sorry."

"Enid, it is fine. We have to get you freed from this. I will be right back. Don't go anywhere until I am back." She motioned for her to stay put as Enid understood, and they both almost laughed at the comment and jester to "stay put."

"Colonel Engels! Dawson!" Geena yelled.

"Over here," he called. He headed to her way with most of his crew and was accompanied by several of the KEBOWS and the prisoner, Karl.

"Colonel, Capo disclosed that their transport ship with reinforcements is already on its way. It is likely too late to intercept it from Earth."

Geena also shared the news about Enid's predicament. A man from the colonel's team followed her back to Enid as Engels began to relay the information to Mission Control. Together, the colonel's team member and Geena effectively freed the relieved Enid. Her face filled with concern, Geena told Enid, "I'm afraid your ankle is broken."

Amazingly, Enid stood and walked about. To their astonishment, her ankle seemed to have healed itself.

Geena heard the prisoners still hashing over their plans when she returned to her listening post. They were more determined to make every effort to escape in time to meet their reinforcements. Glimpsing into the area, Geena saw that Karl had suddenly been led into the group.

Capo shouted at Karl, calling him traitor, and blasted him with challenges. "What have you told them?"

Engels strategy began to work as verbal slurs and arguments hit Geena's ears. Virtually all relevant details were mentally recorded.

—▸◄—

On Moon Mountain, the onslaught of surprise attackers quickly overcame the sentries and guards. Vastly outnumbered, the hideout personnel and guards were swiftly, not so delicately, surprised and captured.

The official report for limited distribution among United States and Russian officials was brief.

> There is currently no spacecraft within the secured area, but evidence that one or more of such ships have left recently. We are in the process of determining details about where such spacecraft might be and how to deal with what we learn.

All were amazed at the sophistication of the equipment inside a mountain, hollowed out and developed into such an inconceivably elaborate reinforced construction. "This is right out of a James Bond movie," one of the troops declared.

With virtually unlimited wealth, it was obvious that Stanislaus had spared little expense with his hideout and efforts.

A virtual global all-points bulletin was issued to locate and apprehend Viktor Stanislaus and those known to have had connections with him. With deliberate care, distinctions between public announcements and the efforts to apprehend the suspected plotters were considered. To minimize public concern, officials decided to keep things as confidential as possible.

The KEBOWS informed the colonel and his men that a spacecraft was about to land. The colonel and his crew scrambled to intercept the craft. Armed and ready, the group, flanked by a hundred angry KEBOWS armed with spear-like weapons, positioned themselves within sight of where the craft most likely would land.

The hatch opened to reveal one person, thought to be the leader, prepared to step onto the surface. Caught by surprise, he and those who followed him were quickly attacked by the colonel's men before they had an opportunity to defend themselves. Fortunately, they had no warning from Capo or anyone else. Some of the group attempted to board their craft, but their efforts were no match. Having been given the order to take no prisoners, almost immediately all fifteen of these enemy reinforcements were shot by the colonel's men.

Mattingly's news from Mission Control to the heads of government and allied agencies involved brought extraordinary relief. Yet as the president of the United States, himself reflected, "We cannot relish true relief until Stanislaus is in captivity or is eliminated."

───⟫◉⟪───

Capo and the remaining prisoners were overwhelmed with the shocking news. They had counted so much on their rescue. Most shared Capo's continued hostility, but a few soon decided to share further knowledge for a trade off for greater food and water and possible kinder treatment, perhaps even their lives.

After the first few hours of animosity and argument, Karl was returned to another area in isolation from the others. He eagerly provided knowledge of their defense and space classified data, particularly pertained to this mission. He told of a United States space scientist with highly classified security clearance who had been selling information to Viktor Stanislaus for huge sums of money. Immediately, Engels directed Henri to inform Mattingly and Mission Control.

Without delay, the FBI located and arrested the previously well-respected scientist as a probable traitor. At the White House, the president responded, "See that all agencies remain on high alert for any possible accomplices. Let's keep the ball rolling.

Find out anything you can from our people on Europedus, no matter how insignificant it might seem."

The representative from NASA replied, "Sir, we have a man constantly in touch with our people there."

GOOD NEWS FROM HOME

"Henri, a spacecraft capable of carrying quite a few people is almost there. Thank goodness, this is one of our own. Weather delays kept the ship from launching earlier. Now these reinforcements will be helpful in cleaning up and in bringing everyone home," Jon reported

"That is great, Jon," Henri responded.

"Please tell Engels to wrap it up and prepare his men...oops... and women—guess I'll have to remember that. Also, the White House authorizes him to use his own judgment regarding the prisoners. The command is to eliminate them if they are a threat to you and the remainder of your mission. They were willing to die for their cause. We may well give them that chance. The White House doesn't want them to remain a threat to the KEBOWS."

Engels and the others were all delighted by the news of reinforcements. The women scientists were especially delighted and in high spirits.

"We have survived eight extremely exciting months! We have learned so much, including learning from our wonderful interactions with the KEBOWS. Look what we've done—we've learned to adapt, survive, and even thrive. And now it's about to end," Marcie said to the scientist's arrest and the possible threat group.

Marcie's summary had pleased each of them, while Geena added, "I believe the best part is living among Enid and her friends. However, don't forget our involvement with a courageous group of protectors. Where would we be if not for Colonel Engels and his men?"

"It's not over yet, ladies," Engels briefed them on the rogue scientist's arrest and the possible threat of further espionage in the United States.

Angela seemed to recall having worked in the same department with the alleged traitor at one time or another during her employment at NASA. "I do remember him fairly well. His name is Harold Watts. He was unusually quiet and private. Where so many talk about family and what they do on time off, he was mum, almost secretive. He did mention a close friend who had moved to the Soviet Union to continue space-exploration research when the United States cut back that priority. I thought at the time that it was an odd thing to say, possibly even lead to a breach of security concern."

"Do you remember a name or where the friend had moved?" Engels asked.

"I do remember overhearing part of a conversation he was concluding on his cell phone. I heard him reply, 'Okay, Koby, keep in touch.'"

"Do you think Koby would be a first or last name?"

"I don't remember why, but I do believe it to be his last name."

"Great. Hmmm. Think, Angela, what else can you remember? Anything at all?"

"Yes, Koby left his family in the United States when he left for Russia. I remember now—Harold mentioned that his friend's wife had a new baby in Florida that he hadn't seen. If anything else jabs my memory, I'll let you know."

"Thanks, Angela, this may be very important."

Angela related all this to Jon at Mission Control. Soon an alert and order to detain was issued for an American man in Russia, who at least at one time, went by the name *Koby*. In a related move, all families with that last name and living in Florida were called, and to the degree possible, interviewed and approached for relevant information.

"We still have to determine what to do with the prisoners. Yes, it is ultimately my decision, but I want your input."

"What do you mean, Colonel?" Geena's respectful voice was subdued and reflected on what she already anticipated.

"This is international terrorism and war," he calmly began. "An execution of all these belligerents is appropriate. Look what they have done and what we have learned they are planning to do."

The women meditated with various degrees of agreement on his logic.

"If it is reasonable to gain more information and they are no longer a threat, as heinous as their crimes and plans are, I would like to see them continued, brought to trial, and incarcerated," Marcie suggested.

Angela simply questioned, "Why? We know that ultimately they will face a death sentence for their parts in all this if brought to trial. Why would anyone want to spend money and effort carting their carcasses around and possibly endangering the lives of all of us in the process?"

When asked, Geena simply stated, "I don't like playing God, but I don't believe these people are in God's favor. I think both of you have very legitimate and valid points. Colonel?"

"I am glad we had this discussion. We will be considering the same things when my men and I have to make the ultimate decision. Ladies, it seems to fall on me."

Reluctantly, all turned to different matters as Engels reflected on his responsibility and evaded further discussion.

—➤●◄—

The KEBOWS seemed to realize that their new friends would soon depart. Many came with gifts of urns made of stone, bundles of tough branches with lance-like leaves, which they politely presented as flowers. Geena recognized the similarity of the branches to some from subtropical America that had a history of being developed into archery and tool handles.

The KEBOW women especially indicated their appreciation of how the Earth women had helped them achieve their freedom and reunification with the males. Enid embraced the three and shared her thanks with remarkable clarity.

Marcie's summary spoke for all three women. "If nothing else comes from this, I'm debating whether catching the bad guys or finding this wonderful tribe of delightful people here is most important. It is ironic to think I have my incarceration to thank for all this opportunity and experience. Most of all, I'm grateful for finding two wonderful friends for life." They understood and affectionately embraced one another as their KEBOW sisters looked on with approval.

The KEBOW men continued to stay nearby, lending support to the colonel's team.   Engels observed, "They don't say a lot, but all seem to have a quick understanding of what to do. They persistently help by any means they can and learn very well. Probably most importantly, they guard the prisoners and take pride in preventing them from hurting their new friends from Earth and, of course, their own people."

"Yes, they are an amazing tribe," Angela agreed as she overheard Engels.

Looking at Engels, the three women started thinking that this was the time where he will reveal his decision regarding the prisoners. He perceived their concern and remarked, "No, I just want us to all start packing for departure."

"What a wonderful sound," Marcie replied, looking at Engels and all the others with obvious gratitude.

"You'll have help loading once the spacecraft arrives, but we need to sort out what we'll need and get organized."

The women scientists shared similar thoughts. Geena thought about going back to Earth and embracing her grandmother to alleviate the concern that she had died in prison or had endured a terrible fate. Marcie dreamt of returning home to her father. She risked wondering to herself whether Harris Connelly might be romantically interested in her, hoping he was, and that she should find out soon.

As they shared their thoughts, Angela simply stated, "I have no one to go back to."

"Angela, you have us!" the two women reminded her.

It's not just the other two women, but Dawson Engels declared quickly and sincerely, "All of us...we have become a family. Angela, we will meet again."

Looking about the lab, the three women began organizing for their departure. Soon several questions arose about whether some of the supplies and equipment would be of assistance to Enid and her people. It was amazing what they had been able to do agriculturally with fairly primitive tools.

"Maybe we can help them with things we have and no longer need," Angela suggested.

"What do you have in mind, Angela?"

"I'm not really sure. Obviously backpacks, containers, things like that. What do you think?"

"Let's bring Enid over and ask what she thinks could be useful," Geena suggested to instant approval.

Henri called out to Geena upon hearing her voice. "Jon Mattingly wants to speak to you."

"Geena, I wanted to let you know as soon as I could that we have obtained clearance for your grandmother in England to become more privy to where you are and what is going on," Jon informed her.

"What?" She was scarcely able to speak. "How did you find her?"

"I did a little detective work on my own and then called in a few markers from some higher ups who owed me some favors. So far, we've told her that you have been on a critical, confidential mission beyond Earth. She didn't believe me until I elaborated about how you were released from prison for this assignment. It took some doing but I convinced her. Mrs. Belcher is a delightful woman. We concluded our conversation by my promising to keep in touch and that she would be hearing directly from you soon."

Initially speechless, Marcie didn't know what to say. Just as Mattingly's concern over the silence had heightened, she gratefully offered, "Jon, you are an amazing person. Thank you! Thank you so much."

"I hope you don't mind that I did this. It was somewhat presumptuous, but word had gotten to me from Warden Post that Mrs. Belcher was growing increasingly anxious about why she had not heard from you. As instructed, the prison personnel remained evasive. You and the crew have already experienced too much danger. It's likely to be necessary to mop up the final details. Colonel Engels will do what is necessary. We trust his judgment.

"Thank you, Jon. We discussed and understood the matter of the prisoners. All three of us are in support of Colonel Engels," Marcie expressed.

"Henri, stay at the controls. We'll head over to the landing site," Colonel Engels ordered.

With three of his men, Engels headed southward to greet the newcomers and guide them back over the desolate terrain.

They arrived virtually the same time as the spacecraft. Engels greeted Commander Connelly, who was the first to alight from the craft, with a professional but friendly salute. It was a very brief degree of formality as Connelly and his crew followed the other four toward the lab.

Time crawled for the women as they waited for Engels and the others to return. Marcie was almost embarrassed by a shortness of breath as she thought of seeing Maj. Harris Connelly again. Finally, after what seemed like the millionth time anyone had looked that way, Geena let the others know. "They're coming."

While Geena's voice was surprisingly composed, Marcie was another story. Breathing deeply, she stood erect with her eyes squinted toward the outlined figures rapidly approaching. Angela mouthed a silent prayer while Enid and a group of the KEBOW aliens stood alert, protecting the women.

Geena, Marcie, and Angela, excitedly rushed to greet everyone from the *Freedom Promise*. Engels noticed how much affection the women shared with the group who had taken them to Europedus. Commander Connelly, Captain Kelly, and Capt. Sean McGraw, were obviously very special to all three women. It was also obvious, however, how much Marcie and Connelly delighted in seeing one another again, although they strived to keep it subdued and low key.

Angela noticed the absence of Tony James, the civilian flight engineer who had accompanied their voyage to the planet. "Tony reluctantly had accepted another assignment and hadn't completed it," Connelly explained.

After their delighted reunion, everyone's attention turned to the mission ahead. "With limited space, we must sort our priorities," Harris Connelly consulted with Dawson Engels. "How many people need to return on this first craft?"

"We have planned to take three women, your prisoner, and two others of your men. What we must do is limit any supplies or other things. Another spaceship will arrive fairly soon to transport the rest of you, the clean up troops we brought with us, and your remaining team."

"That sounds good. Some of the other equipment and materials may be useful to the native creatures of this area, the KEBOWS." Engels went on to explain more about these interesting individuals. "Originally, the name came from Kremlin Ethnos Band of Warriors. Since programmed by Russians, it seemed to fit. Now that name isn't all that appropriate, perhaps, but they don't seem to mind it. It gives them an identity."

Commander Connelly and his group had seen only pictures of this group. He turned his attention with a degree of reserve and appreciation to Enid and offered her a smile and respectful salute. She gracefully returned the salute. Within a few moments, he was representative of the others from Earth in his appreciation of their quick intelligence and adaptability.

"I've been on three previous missions, but this is my first encounter with any life forms that are anywhere this advanced. It's very impressive. My men will have everything under control soon and we will prepare for lift -off."

"Thank you Commander," Engels responded. "I know these three women are more than ready to see Earth again."

"They haven't hesitated to let me know you and your team is the reason they have survived."

"Commander, the spacecraft is ready."

"Thank you, Captain Kelly. Ladies, we're ready to take you home as we promised."

With joyful tears, Geena, Angela, and Marcie bade Engels and those of his men remaining behind a grateful good-bye. It is almost more difficult to leave Enid and the other KEBOWS. Connelly and Engels exchanged salutes in a somewhat formal manner while expressing mutual respect. Henri reported to Jon Mattingly at NASA that they were prepared to board the ship.

Engels put his hand over his heart as he breathed a silent prayer for the safe return to Earth of the craft and his new friends. He turned to see the KEBOWS copying his every move. He was again impressed by how quickly they learned.

———>●●<———

After the excitement of the liftoff, all three women began to share their thoughts with each other.

"Will we be considered heroic space travelers or criminals?"

It wasn't surprising that such would be on their minds, although Geena reminded them that few outside of Mission Control knew their backgrounds. Great effort expended by NASA and the government kept details about their identities from leaking to the public.

On Europedus, Engels, Henri, and the remaining team lost little time preparing for their own return to Earth.

"Colonel, what do you think will happen to those women?" Henri asked.

"Henri, I'm confident that they will be fine. Much depends upon the information disclosed, of course. All three have done a wonderful job in difficult circumstances. They are all amazing women."

"I agree. Even with the ribbing we gave them and all of the physical challenges they faced, they did extremely well. I certainly wish them the best."

"I do as well. Let's get this show on the road and get ready to get out of here when we can before I begin to adapt too much."

"You aren't becoming interested in one of those cute little KEBOW women, are you?"

They both laughed as Engels tapped Henri on the head with his glove.

THE HOMECOMING

Back on Earth, the search widened for Viktor Stanislaus. The more authorities learned about him, the more concerned they had become. Also known as the Devil, his reputation had slowly emerged. Finally, special teams working underground learned that a farmer not far away from Moon Mountain had revealed important information about a secretive stranger buying property, changing the very nature of the area with heavy equipment. Although furnished with few details, this was enough to take focus to that site.

Russian State Security authorities had invited the FBI and Homeland Security teams from the United States to assist. Soon, Special Forces discovered a secret site for rocket launches and a partially concealed entrance to an underground bunker. Moving quickly, they rounded up guards and construction workers in the area. Conspicuously, missing, however, Viktor Stanislaus. All of the equipment quickly confiscated.

The search continued for Stanislaus. The captured workers were too intimidated and terrified to reveal anything—if they knew anything at all. Profiling experts reminded the authorities that it is Stanislaus who was behind the kidnapping threat to the United States president and his family. "A desperate man will do anything and everything, like a cornered animal. He is likely to be very difficult to find," They say.

In Florida, news of a spacecraft's return prompted an unusually large number of people and representatives of the media to Cape Canaveral. Most waited for any sort of specific detail to back up the rampant rumor, opinions, and speculations about this mission to another planet.

Among those in the crowd was Dr. Andrew Adams, one of the few relatives who had been given extensive information about the mission. He was excitedly waiting for his beloved stepdaughter, Marcie. First out of the craft, however, was Commander Connelly, who raised both arms with thumbs up. Among the small group emerging from the spaceship, the appearance of three women caught the quick attention of many in the crowd. More interesting to the crowd, though, were two uniformed astronauts briskly escorting a shackled man away from the crowd.

"Ladies and gentlemen, thank you for coming to this impromptu press conference." Jon Mattingly's voice was professional as the crowd cheered. "Please welcome our crew from an important scientific exploration on another planet. You obviously want more details, and some will be forthcoming. Yet these individuals need time to adjust to our gravity and similar concerns. In addition, each is anxious to spend time with his or her family. We ask for your patience until we are able to provide further information."

An honor guard escorted the crew away from bright flashing lights and an anxious crowd, as questions yelled from the media went unanswered.

Later, there was a knock on Geena's door. She was staying in virtual isolation for almost forty-eight hours, interrupted only by medical and psychological examinations. To her delightful surprise, she fell into the waiting arms of Jon Mattingly. He had been struggling for patience about seeing her since the craft arrived. Their contact and mutual appreciation over the past several months had been primarily nurtured by seeing images of one another on the screen and speaking with each other. Yet it was obvious to both, that their mutual affection had developed into more than a friendship.

"Geena, I'm delighted that you are safe and that you are here."

"Jon, what a wonderful surprise to see you."

"I have a further surprise for you. By the way, you look great." He intentionally concealed his concern that she looked thin, no doubt from her weight loss on Europedus. "Let me give you a few moments to change. I'm taking you to lunch and to the surprise."

"What on earth?" Geena caught herself, "Oh, it is so good to say *earth* again from where I am. Jon, all I have here, is a uniform NASA provided."

"That's fine. You will, and do, look great. I'll pick you up in an hour."

Geena's heart raced as she bathed to get ready. She found a second less-wrinkled NASA uniform. Glancing in the mirror, she agreed the crisp white shirt and khaki trousers flattered her figure. Less-modest honesty would have considered her a stand-out with her golden red hair pulled back in an elegant bun.

As promised, Jon arrived exactly one hour after he left and escorted her to a local restaurant. He had resisted any hint of what the surprise might be. Leading her to a reserved private dining room, Jon opened the door to reveal her grandmother, Sylvia Belcher, from England.

"Oh, I cannot believe this," she sobbed with delight while embracing her beloved grandmother. "Jon, you did this. I'm overwhelmed."

Mrs. Belcher was also speechless and grasped Geena as if she would never let her go. With tears of joy, both women beamed their pleasure to Jon. "Jon, I am eternally grateful.

"Geena, you did something extraordinary for all of us and for your country. We wanted to do something special for you."

The reunion continued as Marcie entered the room with her stepfather, Dr. Adams. A trusted friend from when she worked at NASA accompanied Angela as she joined them. It was hard to separate threads of conversation as all delighted in their reunion together.

⸻

The public learned more, but only in a carefully scripted way. A press release by NASA's Mission Control acknowledged that three brave women were among those on a daring space assignment.

> They were chosen because of scientific expertise and have handled their responsibilities extremely well. These women have demonstrated dauntless courage, encountering unexpected challenges on this mission. There has been a terroristic threat to the United States and other nations of the world which they and others discovered and effectively thwarted.

Although the news articles provided a few other details, not a word mentioned the existence of aliens or the execution of most of the terrorists on Europedus.

Morning newspapers and other media couldn't get enough of the story. Much was made of the scientific specialties of each woman. By mutual agreement, their previous incarcerations were not mentioned in the press. Instead, they were referred as "three incredible scientists."

In the months that followed, there was a wedding engagement announcement of Major Harris Connelly and Dr. Marcie Adams, both astronauts. At the wedding, Geena McBride, escorted by Jon Mattingly, wore a sparkling diamond ring on her left hand.

"It looks like I am destined to be just an old maid," Angela couldn't help but bemoan.

"Angela, you will never be just an old anything," Geena and Marcie simultaneously declared.

⸻

A year passed quickly. The three women had stayed in touch as promised. Angela had returned to the home she received from the will of her generous pastor. She had begun writing a fiction novel under a pen name. She will include tales of aliens and villains. She also lectured frequently. NASA hired her as a specialist and she spoke frequently in their behalf at related colleges and universities.

The three women shared a world unknown to most people. "How many others have shared a life of prison, space travel, and encounters with aliens?" Like a recollected sorority initiation, they laughed at the sheer novelty of it all.

On a recent visit back together, Marcie announced that she and Harris were expecting their first child. "If it is a girl, we plan to name her Enid." Dr. Adams is looking forward to becoming a grandfather.

Geena taught Russian and became a consultant for NASA, with her husband's approval and support. "Not that I need his approval," she quickly reminded her friends. She and Harris were also planning a family.

One early Saturday morning, Angela, awakened right before her usual morning jog, by a knock on the door and peered through the door's eyehole. She could not believe what she saw or, rather, who was outside.

"Are you going to let me in or just glare at me?"

"Col. Dawson Engels," she declared. "I don't believe it. We have been trying to find out just what had happened to you." She decided, he looked just too good. Out of uniform, he was dressed in khaki pants and a fitted black sport shirt.

"I rang your doorbell, but it didn't seem to work."

"We tried to contact you. You missed two weddings."

"I thought I had to be here for the birth of my godchild. Harris contacted me, and of course, I wanted to see you."

"I am so happy to see you."

"I have been so busy on multiple assignments. They won't let me stay in retirement. Remember I told you we would meet again. I've come to ask you to dinner."

Angela was amazed and, no doubt, showed it.

"Now if you don't want to go, I will understand."

"No, not at all. I am honored."

"I'm staying at a downtown hotel. Let's plan on my picking you up at seven this evening."

"How long will you be in town?"

"For once, there is no immediate assignment. I'm flexible."

"Good. Check out, and move into my guest room. We can go to the christening together," Angela offered.

"I'm only willing to do that if you allow me to fix your doorbell." Engels smiled.

When he left, Angela rushed to phone Geena and Marcie with the delightful news.

It was a family reunion at the christening for the twins, Enid and Adam. Many family members, including Mrs. Belcher, who was visiting from England, joined NASA employees, government employees, and friends all celebrating the special occasion and being together.

Angela looked appreciatively at Dawson and whispered affectionately, "Life is good."

Dawson ended up staying at Angela's for three months. During that time, their relationship blossomed from friendship into a shared romantic interest. Their close friends expected it to be a matter of time before they married also.

EPILOGUE

———————— ⟫●⟪ ————————

Dawson Engels startled Angela awake by shaking her at 3:00 a.m. on a Sunday morning. She instantly awakened and saw that he was in full combat gear.

"We're ready to resume our encounters with Viktor Stanislaus. As you know, the search has been ongoing. We have information of where we'll now find him and that is my next assignment."

Angela looked at him with a mixture of love, pride and concern. He had prepared her for this possibility, but still, she was not ready to let him go. "I didn't think you'd be leaving this soon. Please promise me you'll be back safe and soon."

"I will. Especially now I have an incentive."

Their kiss lingered before he reluctantly pulled away after a final hug. Their eyes locked until he disappeared into a military jeep waiting at the curb.

Angela pondered so much, as she watched the jeep as it left the neighborhood. Dawson's orders were classified, but the clues were there.

> The conquest of space has moved ahead with breath-taking speed since the Space Age began October 4, 1957. On that day, Russian scientists launched the first true space traveler, an artificial satellite, called Sputnik. (Harold L. Goodwin)

SYNOPSIS

Dowsing the Universe features three female scientists, each initially incarcerated, who are given an opportunity of spending a year on a foreign planet. Their intelligence and expertise have led to an offer from the United States government, up to the highest level, to offer them exoneration for their crimes after fulfilling a highly classified mission on that planet.

The women learn that a wealthy Russian oligarch, Viktor Stanislaus, is responsible for planning and funding extensive terrorism. The scope of this will threaten that planet Europedus and Earth as well. The three women, challenged to earn freedom and fuller lives and love as they display qualities of courage, bravery, and loyalty.

ABOUT THE AUTHOR

Some materials for this book pertaining to space, prisons, and agencies, such as Interpol, are obtained from articles on the internet.

The author, Barbara Sullivan-Nelson began writing inspirational articles after a career in business management. Through her love of words, she developed a passion to write books. Barbara is the author of *Tracking*, an international thriller, published in 2007, as well as *Ryan's World*, the true story of a special-needs young lady, published in 2011.

Barbara's versatility in writing is leading her ongoing literary projects in many directions as she focuses on another first love—the written word. A native of Middletown, Ohio, Barbara currently resides in Kentucky.